CAROL ROSS

Only Yesterday

By the same author

OUR MOTHER'S HOUSE
A SENTENCE OF LIFE
MAUNDY
A WOMAN OF CHARACTER
SLEEPING DOGS LIE
LOST AND FOUND
BLOOD FOR BLOOD

Only Yesterday

by

Julian Gloag

HENRY HOLT AND COMPANY
New York

First published in the United States in 1987 by
Henry Holt and Company, Inc.,
521 Fifth Avenue, New York, New York 10175.
Originally published in Great Britain

Library of Congress Cataloging in Publication Data
Gloag, Julian.
Only yesterday.
I. Title.
PR6057.L605 1987 823'.914 86-19559
ISBN 0-8050-0131-X

First American Edition

Printed in the United States of America
1 3 5 7 9 10 8 6 4 2

ISBN 0-8050-0131-X

Contents

I	Friday	1
II	Saturday	43
III	Sunday	123

1

Friday

Oliver Darley opened his eyes and blinked slowly as the last wisps of dream dissolved in the dim light of the March afternoon. In the grate, the fire had dwindled to a low mound of ashy lumps laced with a few faint orange threads. The only sound was the high-pitched tick of the long-case clock in the corner of the room.

His eyesight had improved with old age and he hardly ever wore glasses now except for reading. Peering, he made out the form of his wife on the other side of the hearth, her white head bowed in slumber. Abruptly he reached out and switched on his reading lamp. No, not slumber – a telltale cord stretched from her ear to the transistor radio beside her. She was listening in. Darning wool and some of his old socks lay in her lap, but her hands were idle. Suddenly she chuckled.

Oliver stirred restlessly and, marking his place with a pipe cleaner, lifted the blue-bound volume of Surtees from his knees and put it on the table. The old lady chuckled again.

'What are you laughing for?' he asked, his voice still throaty with sleep.

She made no response.

'May,' he said, louder, 'why are you laughing?'

May raised her head and carefully removed the earplug. 'What did you say, dear?'

'I said, when's Miranda due to arrive?'

'In time for tea, she thought – if she could manage it.'

'Tea– filthy muck!'

May smiled faintly and started to replace the earplug.

'It's well past teatime,' he said hastily. 'But then nobody's punctual anymore.'

'That hardly matters to us, Oliver. We're not going anywhere, are we?'

'No, thank God,' he said and then, as the clock gave a preliminary rasp before striking the hour, 'It's almost five – far too late for tea.'

'Not in France.'

'France? We're not *in* France. Anyway, the French are an hour ahead of us. Years ahead of us – in most ways.' He drew a purple handkerchief from his sleeve and blew his nose with a trumpeting flourish.

'And getting too late for my programme,' May murmured.

'Programme? What programme? What are you listening to?'

'The Story Hour, but it wouldn't interest you.'

'Why not? What's it about?'

May sighed. 'If you must know, it's about a young couple with three small children living in Brixton.'

'Why shouldn't it interest me? I was born in Brixton.'

'Yes, dear, but I fancy it's changed quite a bit since your day.'

'*Everything's* changed since my day,' he said with satisfaction, tucking the handkerchief back in his sleeve. 'Not that I. . . .' But the high thin chime of the clock striking the hour overbore him, and by the time it had done, May was plugged in again.

Grunting, Oliver eased himself from the large leather armchair and bent down to the fire. He thrust fiercely at it with the poker, then, using his fingers, picked out half a dozen lumps from the coal scuttle and arranged them on the glowing remnants. He straightened up and wiped his fingers on the seat of his trousers. He was a large man, broad rather than tall, now run to fat in paunch and jowl, but well-dressed, even dapper, in well-cut grey tweeds with pullover, socks and tie of carefully matched purple.

'May,' he said, looking down at her and raising his voice, 'May – I'm going to the studio to make a note.'

Without looking up, she gave him a little wave.

'Might as well be talking to a corpse,' he muttered as he moved towards the door.

Outside, the afternoon rain had let up for the moment. As his taxi drew away, the middle-aged man in a raincoat pushed through the gate and set down his suitcases on the flagstones.

Rupert Darley lit a cigarette and regarded the house in which he had been born and brought up (figuratively speaking – for in fact he'd been born in the City of London Hospital and brought up at a variety of boarding schools in distant counties). For the last several years his occasional visits had been for lunch and he could not remember when he'd last slept there; and yet he still sometimes inadvertently referred to Wisteria Cottage as 'home' – to Sylvia's invariable irritation. He thought wryly that he had left home only to come 'home'. But the relief he had felt in the train coming up – almost elation – that he would never again have to bear the burden of his wife's irritability, her sarcasm, the outright hostility ('If you're going to go, for Christ's sake go!') was overshadowed by a sense of depression at the sight of the place. The house was large by any suburban standard (large enough, in the old days, to house a nanny, a cook and a housemaid, not to speak of a daily gardener-chauffeur and a weekly washerwoman) but its size now seemed merely monstrous. The once immaculate pink wash worn through to the brick in places, the gleaming black shutters grey and flaking, it sat ungainly and diminished in the untended and overgrown garden.

Rupert sighed and took a deep breath of cigarette smoke to cover a sudden stab of pain – of loss or foreboding. In its shabbiness and decay, the house seemed on the point of being overwhelmed by the advancing garden's lush extravagance – and himself along with it perhaps, like some bewildered victim in an Addam's cartoon. He banished the fancy with a smile – he was only staying the weekend.

Behind him, a car went by with a swish of tyres on the wet roadway. A dog barked. He searched for some childhood memory of bliss to push back the present gloom. May, with a basket of spring flowers on her arm, cutting daffodils? But, though he must have watched her doing so a thousand times, he had no picture of it. The only clear memory that came was of Lord, the gardener, stripped to the waist on a brilliant summer's morning, being stung on the throat by a bee from the wisteria. After a minute or two he had sat down on the grass with a dazed look in his eyes, grasping his neck and swallowing convulsively. And Rupert had run into the house and they had laughed at him at first, but then there was flurry and phone calls and he had been sent up to his bedroom where he had watched from the window as the ambulance came and Lord, unconscious now, was put on a stretcher and borne away to the merry ringing of the ambulance bell and the soft murmuration of the maids leaning over the gate.

What had happened to Lord? He'd have to ask May.

Damn. He shouldn't have come.

He could have gone to Milly's. His daughter shared a flat with two other students, but she'd always said she could put him up. ('Don't you *want* to see your old University, Daddy?' It was said ironically of course, because Milly was quite unsentimental about the past. But no, anyway, he did not want to see it – after his first year, the University had become a place of increasing misery for him.) But unless Sylvia had rung her up, Milly hadn't heard the news yet – he'd only written her this morning – and he didn't want any long explanations and dissections (not that Milly cared for that sort of thing either, but some impulse of guilt or justice would force him into it, he knew). Not now, not just yet. He wanted to feel his freedom, breathe it in deeply, get used to it.

He rubbed his cigarette out against the gatepost and put it in his pocket. He bent down and picked up his suitcases and, his shoulders drooping slightly under their weight, walked slowly up the path to the front door.

It had started to rain again.

Oliver blew on his fingers and rubbed his hands together, then picked up a pencil. He was perched on a high swivel stool in front of the drafting board, his feet wide apart for steadiness – and every so often he would rotate slightly to look at the wall on his right. The wall, normally lined with books, was now almost entirely covered by a vast sheet of paper – or several sheets tacked together. Apart from the fact that it was architectural or mechanical, it was difficult in the fading light to decipher the nature of what was drawn on the paper – difficult, that is, for anyone but Oliver, who studied it with grave and familiar calm. He nodded once or twice and murmured something to himself – and the gas fire, turned low, burbled as though in subtle discourse with him.

At that moment the phone rang – Oliver started and dropped his pencil and then, standing, stepped on it and broke it.

'Hell and damn!' He took a couple of steps to the desk and picked up the phone. 'Seven-five-four three-two-one-five,' he roared, holding it well away from his ear, and without pause, 'seven-five-four three-two-one-five!' He slammed down the receiver. 'Bloodstained instrument.'

He stood, panting slightly, and glancing vaguely round the studio. It was a large room made small by the quantity of professional furniture – filing drawers, built-in cupboards, drafting cabinets, racks, long tubes of flaking leather, even the single armchair was piled with papers and books. It had not been tidied for years, and Vi was only allowed in once a month, under strict supervision, to dust and vacuum – but it was the disorder of fundamental order and Oliver could have laid his hand on a paper clip in the dark.

He bent down and retrieved the broken pencil and dropped it into the wicker waste-paper basket. He paused, getting his breath, then picked up the waste-paper basket and switched off the little light above the drafting board.

Rupert arrived outside the studio window just as his father was leaving the room.

He had rung the front doorbell twice, and both times had waited three or four minutes – it could easily take that long for Oliver to respond and longer for May. He had circled the house, stopping at the sitting room window and waving vigorously, but May's radio armoured her invincibly against intrusion and even his gentle tapping had not roused her. So he had come round at last to the studio, only to see Oliver vanish.

He laughed with rueful exasperation – this could go on for quite some time. The house was locked and double locked and manacled with chains – as secure as a fortress, with no loophole or half-open scullery window through which he might squeeze. In his youth he had often shinnied up a pipe and got in through the bathroom window, but he was hardly up to that these days. Once, not so very long ago, he'd been forced to go down to the Prince Albert and ring them up from there.

He went back to the side of the house and, stepping carefully on the border, placed himself at the West window where he could catch May's eye if she were looking. He hesitated to rap on the pane – sudden noises always alarmed the old man.

Oliver was standing on the hearth rug facing May, holding the waste-paper basket with solicitude, like an acolyte with some sacred offering. He was evidently 'holding forth', as May would put it, and she regarded him with a familiar look of weary attentiveness.

Cold as he was in the miserable drizzle, Rupert watched without moving – he was not eaves-dropping for he could hear nothing that was said and, even if he could, it would be trivial. Once or twice Oliver picked a scrap of paper from the basket, then cast it back; May fitted the heel of a sock over the darning mushroom; otherwise, the scene was static. Yet the soundlessness added a curious sense of secret drama – Rupert's detachment made sudden strangers of them, their words foreign, their thoughts unguessable. The thin glass barrier set him apart and untouchable, the ignorant and guilty voyeur outside looking in.

He pressed close against the window and raised a hand and waved.

'I don't *know* who it was – some lunatic or other.'

'What did he say, dear?'

'Nothing. The bloody thing just beeped at me.'

'Somebody ringing from a call box – you have to *wait* a few seconds, Oliver. I expect it was Miranda, she said she might ring when she got in.'

'Damnation! Didn't *you* hear the phone?'

'No, dear, I was listening to the news. I shouldn't worry – she's bound to try again. She's a sensible girl.'

'I'm perfectly well aware she's a sensible girl – though God knows where she got it from. Skipped a generation, I suppose. Well, I'd better go and empty the –'

'Hello,' said May, looking over the top of her glasses, 'there's someone at the window.'

'Who? Where?' Oliver turned and caught sight of a waving hand and the vague outline of a face. 'Christ, so there is! May, call the police at once.'

'Don't be so silly. Why, I do believe it's Rupert.'

'You mean Miranda.'

'Don't you recognize your son?'

'Rupert?'

'Do you have any others? Go and let him in.'

'What in the name of God is he doing here?'

'He's coming to stay for a few days. I told you. He rang up this morning. Don't tell me you've forgotten?' Smiling, May nodded and signalled at Rupert to go round to the front door.

'Bugger. Of course I haven't forgotten. But why he should choose this weekend of all weekends is beyond my –'

'Oh for pity's sake, let him *in*. It's pouring with rain out there.'

'Alright alright.' He started to move. 'Coming!' he bellowed uselessly.

'Hello, Oliver.'

'Oh hello.' Oliver supported himself with one hand on the door and the other on the jamb, effectively blocking the entrance. Two bolts, a Chubb, a Yale, and a chain – opening the front door was an exhausting task. 'How long have you been out there?'

'Only five or ten minutes,' Rupert said cheerfully, picking up his suitcases.

'You shouldn't hang about in this weather. It's bitterly cold out today – the wind's from the Northeast.' He opened the door wider and peered out past Rupert as though at a foreign country. 'I suppose you'd better come in.'

'Thanks.' Rupert stepped over the threshold and dumped his bags by the stairs.

Oliver eyed them dubiously. 'How long are you proposing to stay?'

'Not long.' Rupert smiled. 'Just a few nights. Don't worry – I'll be gone by the holiday.'

'Holiday?'

'Easter, you know. Next week.'

'Christ.' Oliver banged the door and set to work relocking it. 'We were expecting Miranda,' he said over his shoulder.

'Milly? Is she coming? Well, that is a surprise.'

'Not to me. I invited her.'

'I see.' He draped his raincoat over the banister and looked at himself in the heavily gilt hall mirror. His thinning grey curls had been flattened by the rain; he started to dry his hair with his handkerchief. In the glass he saw his father staring intently at him with the same sort of steady look he gave to objects of architectural or artistic interest. It was not unkindly meant, but Rupert glanced away – it reminded him too strongly of the intense gaze Sylvia would sometimes direct at him before making some oracularly dotty remark. Sylvia – dotty? Such a judgement would never have occurred to him a few weeks ago, even a few days ago.

He put away his handkerchief and turned slowly. 'Well now – how are you?'

'Damned old.' Oliver moved over to the hallstand where the waste-paper basket was perched precariously. 'I don't mind telling you this weather gets me down. My fingers are so stiff I can hardly rule a straight line. It takes me two weeks to do what I could have done in a day twenty years ago.'

'Well – spring's on the way.'

'Spring?'

'I think Monday will be the first day of spring, won't it?'

'I haven't the faintest idea.'

'Ummm. Tell me, how's the Pyramid coming along? It must be nearly finished – I'm longing to see it built.'

'Built? My dear boy, it will never be *built* – not in my lifetime. Or yours. Where do you imagine the money would come from? Now your mother wants me to fork out for a stairlift.'

'One of those little chairs that goes up and down on a rail?'

'Exactly. I've had an estimate – four thousand pounds.'

'Good Lord, that's a bit steep.'

'The blasted rail must be cast in gold.'

'Still, if it'll make things easier for May, it will be money well spent.'

'Money you don't have can never be well spent.' He took hold of the waste-paper basket. 'You'd better go in and see her.'

'Yes. How is she?'

'As well as can be expected. There's nothing you can do about old age. She feels the cold as much as I do – more, probably. Although she doesn't complain about it like me. But then, unlike me, your mother's a Christian – more or less. She'll be pleased to see you.'

'Right. You coming?'

'No, I'm going to empty this in the dustbin. And if I were you, I'd hang that mackintosh up in the cloakroom, it's dripping all over the floor.'

As Rupert hung up the coat, he heard Oliver in the kitchen rattling the bolts of the back door, his voice uplifted in song:

> . . . eighty in the shade they say,
> Really very hot for May –
> Oh what very charming weather!

The old boy was in better spirits.

May's hand was dry as paper, but her cheek was soft as peach bloom.

'This is a pleasant surprise,' she said as he kissed her.

'A bit spur of the moment, I'm afraid.'

'That doesn't matter. Now sit down and tell me all your news.' She pointed at the red leather poufe beside her chair. 'How is Sylvia?'

'Sylvia? Oh – she's alright.' He sat awkwardly on the poufe, which was too low for his length of leg, but it had always been the place of honour and intimacy. 'She's busy lecturing, you know, as well as reviewing – and of course she's getting on with her book.' He took out his cigarettes and lit one.

'What is it about, I don't recollect?'

'Medea – the myth and the play. Literary anthropology, I suppose you'd call it – from a rather specialized feminist point of view, I gather, although I've only been allowed to see bits of it.' He had come here to tell May that he'd left his wife, and yet when it came to the point he was engaging in this automatic babble, of no conceivable interest to her.

'How interesting. Is Medea the same as Medusa? I'm afraid I always get them muddled up.'

Rupert laughed, half-choked on his cigarette, laughed again. 'No – not the same. Medea killed her own children. Medusa's the one who turned you to stone if you looked at her.'

'Oh yes, rather like Lot's wife. Dear me, what an exceedingly unpleasant subject.'

Rupert glanced quickly at her, but her air of innocence was inviolate. 'Yes, not very nice.' He smiled and felt better. 'But, listen, how are you?'

'Oh, you know – I have my good days and my bad days. But they're all spent fastened to this wretched chair.' She threaded the needle and began to darn – the wool she used was a shade darker red than the sock, Rupert noticed.

'You're not getting out to the garden at all?'

'The garden?' She gave him a straight look. 'Have you *seen* the garden?'

'Yes – it is a bit out of control, I suppose.'

'A jungle. It sends shivers down my spine. No, not the garden, thank you very much,' she said – she who had lavished years, decades of careful love on border and bed and bush. There were no flowers in the room. Rupert's heart smote him – the least he could have done was to have bought a bunch of irises or freesias at Waterloo.

'. . . as much as I can do to hobble into the kitchen – though to tell you the truth I don't care much for the kitchen these days. I find the sight of food rather sickens me.'

'What do you eat then?'

'I rather rely on bread and milk – that's something dear old Vi can't get wrong. And my bran of course.' She nodded at her small table cluttered with books and boxes, the phone, her radio, and a large jar of wormlike brown bran among the innumerable bottles of pills. 'It's supposed to help my digestion, I think.'

'And what are all the pills for?' Rupert stood up and flicked his ash into the fire.

'I couldn't begin to tell you, my dear – except for the painkillers of course.'

'But at least they work?' He idly picked up the poker and weighed it in his hand.

'Not as well as they did – they seem to be losing their force. I'm not supposed to take more than two every six hours, but that simply isn't enough.'

'I don't imagine it would do any harm to take an extra one or two now and again.' He began to jab at the fire.

'Well of course that's just what I do, but it worries me all the same. I keep meaning to ask Dr Bowson. As a matter of fact he was here earlier in the week, but I forgot again. I shouldn't do that if I were you, dear, Oliver doesn't like his fire being interfered with.'

'Oh – of course not. Sorry.'

'You needn't apologize to me. It's just one of his things, like locking up and emptying the rubbish.'

'Yes – that's what he's doing now.'

'He positively haunts the dustbin – you'd think it contained the crown jewels the way he carries on. And lately he's taken to muttering in the night. "Pyramid," it was last night – "pyramid, pyramid", over and over again.'

Rupert dropped his cigarette into the fire. 'How's the Pyramid coming along, by the way? He was a bit cagey about it when I asked him just now.'

'He knows better than to talk to me about that blasted thing.'

'Why?'

May glanced up with a frown that carried all the severity of the classroom. 'Why what?' she said.

'I mean, why shouldn't he talk to you about it – after all, architecture is his life, isn't it?'

'And very nice for him, I'm sure.' May bent her head to her darning. 'Personally I've never been able to see what all the fuss is about. I mean I'm very fond of St Paul's and the National Gallery, but I shouldn't wish to stand and look at them all day. I think architecture should be about people first and then . . . .'

Rupert lit another cigarette – in his inner ear he seemed to hear Sylvia's voice, the sharp fingers of her intellect briskly crumbling the small stale loaves of wisdom he'd stored up against the day of famine. What nourishment was left to him?

'. . . decent-sized and well-lit kitchens with shelves at the proper height, but what makes you think your father knows anything about people?'

Rupert blinked. 'What does he talk to you about then?'

'Mainly about where he's going to be for the next five minutes – or where he's been. Sometimes I think he's quite potty, the poor old boy. I mean, as if I *care*.'

'Perhaps he really wants to make sure of where *you* are.'

May cocked her head to one side considering. 'Yes, I think you might be right.' She nodded. 'I say, Rupert, *apropos* of that, I'll tell you a funny story.'

Rupert took a seat on the couch. 'What's that?'

'It was early on Monday morning, I think. He got up to go to the bathroom – as he does about twenty times a night. And it isn't like any ordinary person getting out of bed, you know. He puffs and pants and groans and stamps and damns and blasts – a regular carry-on. And of course he woke me up – but I pretended to be asleep. Then *I* got up and went into the little bedroom to make myself a cup of tea with the electric kettle you gave me. When I got back he was sitting on the end of his bed sobbing. "Why, whatever is the matter, Oliver," I said. "I thought you were dead," he said, "I was sure you were dead." Well now, what do you make of that?'

'He had a shock.' He remembered once when Milly was four or five, coming in late and going straight up to kiss her goodnight – and finding the form in the bed was not Milly but a carefully arranged bolster. Sylvia had neglected to tell him she was sleeping at a friend's house, and Milly herself had had the idea of the bolster so that he wouldn't be sad that she was gone. Yet he'd never forget that first moment of throat-catching panic. 'What did you say?'

'I didn't know what to say at first. I mean I was so obviously not dead – more's the pity. Then I told him he should have looked at my ears and if they were still pink that meant I was alive. Then he said, "But I couldn't see your ears, they were covered by the sheet." Now I ask you!'

'Ummm. Apart from that, how has he been on the whole?'

'He had one of his attacks three or four days ago, but he seems alright now.'

'Is that why Dr Bowson came?'

'Not really. He came to see me.'

'Oh?' He sat up straighter. 'Why?'

May paused in her darning. 'Well, I don't want to bother you with it, my dear. As a matter of fact, I'm planning to have a little chat to Miranda about it. I've asked her for the weekend, you know.'

'*You've* asked her? But I thought Oliver said –'

'With her specialized knowledge, I'm sure she'll make it all quite clear to me.'

'Good heavens, May, Milly's only in her fourth year of medicine – she doesn't know everything.'

'Who does, my dear?' said May sweetly. 'But she's such a sensible young woman and so downright. Just like her mother. The downrightness, I mean.'

'She'll grow out of that, with any luck.' He got up and dropped some ash into the fire. 'After all, nothing's ever really happened to her yet.'

'I suppose you could say nothing's ever happened to me either.'

Rupert smiled. 'Plenty of things have happened to you. You had a child, for one thing.'

'Oh yes.' She held the sock up to the light to examine the darn. 'But I thought you were talking about unpleasant experiences.'

'Was I?' He nodded slowly. 'Yes, perhaps I was.'

'And you've had rather more than your fair share of unpleasantness, haven't you? All those unsatisfactory wives. . . .'

'Oh come on, drat it,' he forced a smile, 'I've only had two.' He stood staring down at her – in her mauve wool dress with a boule brooch at the neck and a mauve shawl about her shoulders, she looked as mild as a dove; only the firm line of the mouth and the jut of the acquiline nose hinted at something more formidable. The darn had proved satisfactory and she was starting on another sock – a bright blue one with yellow heel and toes.

'May,' he said slowly, 'there is something I should perhaps tell you.'

'If you're quite sure, dear.' She looked up at him with a faint smile. 'Otherwise, these things are sometimes better left unsaid. I remember my father always used to say that –'

The phone interrupted her; she laid down her sewing and picked it up.

'Damn,' Rupert murmured, yet he was conscious of a sense of relief.

'Seven-five-four three-two-one-five . . . Miranda, my dear, how nice to hear your voice. Was it you that rang a little earlier?'

Milly – there was no way out of it, he was going to have to tell her this weekend too. He raised his eyes. The rain thrashed quickly against the window panes, and in the garden the bushes were being buffeted by the wind – dark, squat shapes in the dusk, struggling to get loose. There was no sign of a let-up. In the local train coming down, there had been a sudden rift in the clouds and for a few moments a brilliant rainbow had spanned the green gleaming stretch of Barnes Common. He had turned from the window at the same instant as the woman sitting opposite and they had exchanged smiles as sudden and brilliant as the rainbow. She was an ordinary woman, they had said nothing, but momentarily so beautiful that he had been washed by a tide of quiet desire. He had got out at the next station, but she had travelled on.

'. . . well, my dear, of course you must. I expect I'll be in bed by the time you arrive – in which case we'll have our little chat in the morning. Your father's here, do you want a word with him? Very well, my dear, goodbye then.' She put down the receiver. 'Miranda sends you her love. She's going to be a little late. Something about a friend who's in some kind of trouble. Archie something – who would that be?'

'I don't know.' He sighed. 'Another of Milly's lame ducks, I expect.'

'I don't see why you should sigh. Some of us lame ducks have good cause to be grateful to the Mirandas of this world.'

Rupert shrugged and sat down in Oliver's armchair. 'May – what's all this about? Why did Bowson come and see you?'

'Well, dear,' she said, taking off her glasses, 'if you must know, it's to do with regulating my pills. And he wants me to have a course of physiotherapy – for my knees. I gather this means I should have to go into hospital for a week or two.'

'Hospital?' He made a sharp movement that dribbled ash down his shirtfront. 'But, good heavens –'

'Oh dear – don't *you* go on at me about it!'

'Oh. I'm sorry.' He paused. 'Has Oliver been going on at you?'

'I haven't told him yet – but I expect he will. Which is why I feel I'll need some moral support when I do tell him.'

'I see. From Milly, I suppose?'

'He has a great respect for your daughter, Rupert – and he does listen to what she says.'

Rupert laughed abruptly and stubbed out his cigarette in Oliver's ashtray. 'It's getting dark. I'd better draw the curtains.'

Oliver sat down with a grunt. 'Who was that on the phone just now?'

'Miranda.'

'Ah. I'm very fond of that girl.' He looked at his table, patted the matchbox, tapped the tobacco jar, picked the cigarette stub out of the ashtray and flung it in the fire. 'Where is she? Why isn't she here?'

'She's at King's Cross – she'll be coming after dinner.'

'Hell's teeth – who'll see to the locking up?'

'Don't worry,' Rupert said, 'I'll look after that.'

'Do you know how?'

'Of course I do.' He paused to get the timing right, then chimed in with his father:

'The keys are in the brass box on the hallstand,' they said as one and, together, laughed.

'Oh that reminds me, Oliver – I've brought you a bottle.'

'A bottle of what?'

'Laophraiog. I went over to Islay for a few days at half-term last month, and I picked up a rather special bottle of malt. I think you'll like it.'

'Islay – in February? You must be mad – or damnably hardy.'

'It was a bit chilly, I must admit. But I got in a good bit of climbing. Hold on, I'll fetch it.' He started towards the door.

'Get a jug of water while you're about it, there's a good chap. And you might move your bags from the bottom of the staircase, they're a positive deathtrap where they are.'

'I'll take them upstairs. Er, May – where shall I be sleeping?'

'I had Vi make up your old room for Miranda – she usually has it when she comes. So perhaps you'd better take the spare room over Oliver's studio, the one with green curtains. You'll find sheets in the linen cupboard.'

'Frank Lloyd Wright slept there when he stayed, so you'll be in good company.'

'No, Oliver, that dreadful daughter of his slept in that room – *he* had the pink room.'

'If you say so.'

'I do say so.'

'Very well, very well – have it your own way, my dear,' he said, giving his son a surreptitious wink.

The room with green curtains was not inviting. The walls were green, too, of a sickly yellowish tone, with a damp stain on the ceiling. There were cardboard boxes on the floor, a kitchen alarm clock with the glass cracked, and framed prints from the Natural History Museum – of grasses and mushrooms and faintly menacing plant life.

Rupert lugged his cases onto the bed. He found the whisky and a hairbrush and quickly brushed his hair in front of a dulled and spotted mirror that reflected an image obscure and murky with time.

At the head of the stairs he stopped – and then turned into his old bedroom. He switched on the light. It was warm; someone had lit the gas and drawn the curtains – Oliver of course. The cream-coloured wallpaper with little swags and urns of flowers was unchanged. Above the fireplace was a blown-up photo of a small boy in a polo-necked sweater and blazer and shorts; he stood on top of a flat-topped brick structure – like a huge square bollard – on a stony beach. He had his legs apart and his right arm raised high above his head, with a smile on his lips and his curly hair blowing in the wind, in the classic stance of young hero leading the troops or conquering the heights.

Rupert gave him a quick smile of recognition and then knelt on the bed under the window and drew back the curtain. The nursery bars were still in place. From here, on a clear day you could see right across the Park to the distant hills of Surrey – and watch the deer rutting in the autumn and the jodphured girls in their little velvet caps cantering along the tracks. Here too he had lain waiting at night until the sweep of the car's headlights across the ceiling signified the return of Oliver and May from one of their parties. Once he'd woken in the morning to find a huge plush giraffe beside him, which they'd won at some nightclub.

He let the curtain drop. There was nothing to see now.

The stout oak bookcase he'd inherited from May's father, who'd made it himself from coffin board and used it for unread volumes of nineteenth-century sermons. It still housed the remnants of Rupert's once prized library: Harrison Ainsworth, Dornford Yates, Poe, *Virginibus Puerisque*, *The Infamous John Friend*, Marryat, *London Belongs to Me*, *Handy Andy*, C. H. B. Kitchin, Henry Green, *A Treasury of Light Verse*, Ogden Nash, *The Path to Rome*, *Reynard the Fox*, *The Cloud of Unknowing* . . . and what was this? *Selected Poems of John Crowe Ransom*. Rupert pulled it out of the shelf – he'd thought it lost or lent decades ago. He opened it and read for a minute or two and smiled –

> Away went the messenger's bicycle,
> His serpent's track went up the hill forever,
> And all the time she stood there hot as fever
> And cold as any icicle.

Who else could have found a rhyme for bicycle without appearing ridiculous? Still smiling, he turned a page and read on. . . .

Oliver picked up a silver snuffbox, opened it, sniffed at it, then put it back on the table. 'A malt! I detest malt whisky – I should have thought he'd have known that by now.'

'I'm sure he meant well, dear.'

'They're the most dangerous of the lot – the people who "mean well". The untold harm that good men do.'

'Surely you wouldn't want the world run by bad men?'

'I'd like to see Rupert running the world – he can't even run his own life. He's never stuck to anything for more than five minutes.'

'He's been a schoolmaster for a number of years now.'

'That doesn't count – anyone can be a school teacher.'

'I was one myself, if you remember,' she said tartly.

'That's quite different – you didn't have much option as a woman in those days if you wanted to earn your own living.'

'And so was my father.'

'A *head* master – and a damned good one. But he gave it up soon enough when he was offered the living in – Christ, who's been mucking about with the fire?'

'I asked Rupert to give it a poke – it seemed to be dying.'

'And now it's bloody nearly dead.' He heaved himself out of the chair and went down on one knee, muttering as if to himself, but in fact quite audibly. 'Damned smokeless fuel – useless stuff.' He carefully positioned a few lumps, then rammed them with the poker. 'Might as well feed the fire with cow pats. All this pollution nonsense – what's wrong with a good old-fashioned pea-souper, I'd like to know?'

May said, 'It's rather like the starlings.'

'What?' Still on one knee, he turned to look at her. 'What are you saying?'

'Starlings.'

'Starlings? What starlings? What on earth are you talking about?'

'Everyone's fond of birds,' she said tranquilly, 'but something had to be done about the starlings in Trafalgar Square, didn't it, because they were defacing the buildings? And we all like a roaring log fire, but it poisons the atmosphere, doesn't it? – and actually asphyxiates people.'

'Ugh.' Oliver pulled himself to his feet. 'There are too many damned people in the world as it is.' He let the poker drop with a clang. 'Where the devil's Rupert? I could do with a drink.'

'Hazel Maybury has left off sugar and says it has done wonders for her.'

'Don't you believe it.' Oliver lifted his glass and smelled the whisky. 'Nothing short of divine intervention could do anything for that silly bitch.'

'I don't see why you call her a bitch just because she thought Le Corbusier was the name of a brandy.'

'That's why I call her silly. I call her a bitch because she shouts at poor old Maybury from the bedroom window.' He pulled his face down and gave a falsetto shriek, '*Geoffrey!*'

Rupert laughed and took a mouthful of malt – savouring its seaweed-scented delicacy.

'You're jolly lucky I don't shout at you sometimes,' May said sharply.

'I know I am, my dear. I am perfectly aware of that. I am one of the luckiest men alive. Your mother, Rupert, has the patience of an angel.'

'Oh tsch!'

'But you have, my love, you have! And I am one of the most intolerant and impatient of men,' he said mellowly. 'Particularly now that I've given up smoking. Rupert, did I tell you I'd given up smoking? Completely lost the taste for it – just like that!' He snapped his fingers. 'Gone mit der rose und der nightingale!'

'Then it's a good thing I didn't bring you cigars instead of the Laophraiog. How is it by the way?'

'Delectable, my boy, quite delectable! But cigars are always useful for bribing the dustmen, you know. One has to bribe the working class to do what they used to do with a cheerful smile and a tip of the cap in the old days.'

May sighed over her darning. 'Please, Oliver – *not* politics.'

'That's not politics, my dear – that's simple, corrupt human nature. I expect when the ambulance men come to take me away at the last, they'll have to be given a few glasses of my best sherry – or your La Frog, Rupert – before consenting to cart the corpus from the premises.'

May said, 'The ambulance men are on strike.'

'All the more reason to bribe them – common form in banana republics, I believe, and we're not much above that level these days. What was that banana republic you were in, Rupert?'

'You mean the year I spent in Venice?'

'No no – *not* Italy – the Italians still retain a few vestiges of respect for culture. That other place.'

Rupert frowned. 'Germany? No, oh I know – that time I did those guided tours of Macchu Picchu?'

'That's it – Chile.'

'Peru actually.'

'Chile, Peru, England – there's virtually no difference these days. God knows what we'd do if there was a war.'

'There wouldn't be time to do much. Anyway, according to that American general, our armed forces are just a collection of bands and admirals.'

'I may be pretty far gone, my boy, but not so far gone as to agree with some bum-faced American general.'

'Why does it always have to be bum?' May gently enquired.

'Because the face looks like a bottom – and they wipe it with toilet paper.'

'Kleenex, I think you'll find,' said Rupert.

'I expect you're right. Nasty little pieces of paper filled with snot. Civilization began with the handkerchief and ended on –'

'August the fourth, nineteen fourteen,' Rupert got in on cue.

'Precisely.' Oliver took a cautious sip of the malt. 'Although I still retain a great respect for the Royal Navy.'

'Rupert, I'm afraid I shall have to trouble you to look after the dinner this evening, if you don't mind.'

'Yes, sure – I'd be delighted.'

'Can you cook?' asked Oliver.

'In a manner of speaking. I took it up when Sylvia got her first job – that's a long time ago now.'

'Well, that's alright then.'

'There's steak – two quite nice pieces of fillet. And Vi will have peeled some potatoes – they should be in a pan on the stove.'

'Bread and milk for you?'

'Yes please. And I think perhaps I shall have an apple.'

'An apple, right.' He stood up. 'I'd better get things started.'

'Plenty of time, my boy, plenty of time, no need to rush off.'

'Aren't you hungry?'

'I'm always hungry.'

'In that case . . . .'

'Well, fill yourself up before you go.'

'Perhaps I shall. What about you?'

'Not for me, thanks.' Oliver laid a protective hand over his glass. 'I have to watch my alcoholic intake, you know.'

'*Watch* is the right word,' murmured May.

Rupert went over to the black oak coffin chest on which the drinks were kept and poured a large shot of malt into his rummer. 'What should I do for a vegetable, May?'

'Don't use any of the fresh vegetables – they're for the weekend. You might find some frozen peas in the freezer – otherwise, you can open a tin of baked beans.'

Rupert turned round. 'Baked beans with steak?'

'Oh we're not fussy about that sort of thing these days.'

Rupert glanced at Oliver, but the old man had judiciously closed his eyes.

'Baked beans it is, then.' He raised his voice. 'How do you like your steak?'

Oliver opened his eyes. 'Bloody. Let my thoughts be bloody and my deeds be bold, as Queen Victoria said to the Archbishop of Canterbury.'

Rupert laid his hand on the door.

'Oh, and Rupert.'

'Yes?'

'You might open a bottle of wine – there's some of the Society's Beaune left, I think, which should be quite drinkable.'

As soon as Rupert had gone, Oliver shut his eyes tight, raised his glass, and drained the malt. 'Ugh,' he muttered, 'filthy muck.'

'. . . a ridge of high pressure moving across Northern France is expected to reach the South Coast by early morning. The regional forecast for South and South-East England: clear, sunny skies with unseasonably high temperatures likely to range from a low of seven to a high of nineteen degrees Celsius, that's forty-five to sixty-six fahrenheit. In the South-West –'

Rupert leaned over and switched off the radio – next would be the news, and he hadn't the least desire to hear the news. Next week – soon – he would pack up and leave for some place where the only news would have the eccentric charm of all foreign local events – whispered scandals in high places, angry fruit-growers storming town halls, bishops dying of heart attacks in brothels, terrific hail storms, bizarre railway accidents, monstrous eating contests. . . .

He lit a cigarette and opened the back door to let out the ancient cooking smells. Letting in the fresh air – he'd done a lot of that already today. He'd had his last meal at the club and handed in his resignation to the Secretary directly afterwards – always a ridiculous expense; he'd visited the school and collected the last of his books from the common room; he'd written a letter to Milly and posted it, and another to Sylvia and left it propped on the mantelpiece; he'd phoned May, packed his bags, tickled the cat under the chin, and shut the front door behind him for good and all. Also, for some reason he couldn't quite explain, he'd drawn two hundred pounds from the bank. And he'd smiled at an unknown woman on a train – the Rainbow Lady.

He drained the potatoes and took them out to mash in the backyard where the night air would fluff them up. Several cars passed – suburbanites returning home to weekend domesticity. There were no lights in the Mayburys' house. The rain had stopped.

Salt, pepper, butter, milk – he beat them in with brisk, vigorous strokes – and an ash-dropping from his cigarette. He beat that in too.

Oliver hummed softly, taking an occasional sip from his whisky – the blended variety.

'What's holding Miranda up?' he asked suddenly.

May looked up from her book – the darning had been put away. 'She has to go and see a friend.'

'Oh yes?' He rubbed a finger meditatively across his lips. 'Friend, eh? Pretty girl, Miranda.'

'That's got nothing to do with it. Rupert says it's a lame duck.'
'Dog.'
'What about dogs?'
'The idiom is lame *dog*. Lame duck is an American expression relating to someone finishing out a term of office, to the succeeding term of which someone else has or will be elected.'
May went back to her book for a moment, then raised her head again. 'All the same, I'm sure Rupert said lame duck.'
'Rupert is not invariably accurate in his use of language, despite the fact that he once wrote a brilliantly funny book.'
'The one about the end of the war?'
'To my knowledge he has only written one book.'
'Was it really so funny? I couldn't raise a smile. To tell you the perfectly honest truth, I thought it was beastly.'
'War is beastly.'
'Then why does one have to write about it?'
'Because that's what *art* is all about.'
'I don't think I understand about art.' She glanced at the page before her. 'Is Georgette Heyer art?'
'Georgette Heyer is most certainly not art. Georgette Heyer is *trash*!'
'Then what about Jane Austen?'
'Jane Austen is the genuine article.'
'I've never liked her.'
'That's neither here nor there. I've never liked her either – but then I don't like women writers.'
'You liked that P. D. James I lent you last week.'
'P. D. James isn't a woman.'
'She most certainly is.'
'Good God!'
May gave him a little smile. He breathed out heavily, a mournful expression on his face.
'I wish to hell I hadn't given up smoking.'

'This is all very grand,' said May, wincing briefly as she sat down. 'I see you've put out the Scroggs silver.'

'Was that wrong?' Rupert took her cane and hung it on the back of her chair.

'Oh no. But we generally have our meals on our laps these days. We only use the dining room when we have company and Vi's here to serve.'

'Well, I'm company of a sort, I suppose.'

'Of course you are, my boy,' Oliver said, helping himself lavishly to mashed potatoes. 'And damned good company too.'

'Oh, drat it,' said May, 'I've forgotten to take my pills. Rupert, I wonder if I could trouble you to –'

'No you haven't, my dear – you took them about ten minutes ago.'

'Are you sure?'

'I saw you swallow them with my own eyes. What's this? Brussels sprouts – frozen, I suppose?'

'Then perhaps I'm not as silly as I think I am.' She took a small spoonful of bread and milk.

'I see you've opened the wine, Rupert. You'll have to manage that bottle by yourself. It's no good to me. I've completely lost my palate for the stuff. I shall stick to whisky.' He began to eat rapidly.

They were all at some distance from one another, for the dining room table doubled as a billiard table – along with the heavy Victorian chairs and the large two-tiered sideboard covered with badly carved swags of fruit and vegetables, it had been transported bodily from the old rectory when May's father had died, displacing the elegant Regency furniture Oliver had picked up for a song in his younger days. Sipping his wine, Rupert regarded it all with nostalgia, ugly as it undoubtedly was; he had none but happy memories of the rectory.

'Rupert,' May said, 'did Oliver tell you we're going to have a stairlift installed?'

'He did mention it, yes.' He glanced at Oliver, whose attention seemed to be solely devoted to the food. 'I rather thought it was still in the planning stage.'

'Oh did you?' May said cheerfully. 'Of course, it's going to be rather expensive – but it's no good thinking about money when something essential has to be done, is it?'

'In theory, I suppose not, but –'

'As it is, I can only just manage the stairs – once down, once up, every day.'

'Quite – but surely you'd be eligible for a special disability grant?'

Oliver stopped eating. 'What's that?'

'Well, disabled people do have the right to grants for expenses – even quite major ones – which are essential for their health and well-being. Of course, it's apt to take rather a –'

'You mean a handout from the State?'

'I'm not sure if it comes from the DHSS or the local authority, but –'

'If you think I'm going down on my knees to some half-baked bloody little bureaucrat, you can think again.'

May sighed and pushed aside her half-finished bread and milk.

'There must be other possible solutions.'

'Such as what, dear?' May was peeling an apple with a small silver fruit knife. Oliver's head was down.

'Let's forget about the stairs for a moment. Suppose you made the downstairs cloakroom into a bathroom – there wouldn't be space for an actual bath of course, but didn't you tell me some time ago that you weren't taking baths anymore, May? And there'd certainly be room for a shower or a bidet – not very expensive to instal – and you've already got the washbasin and lavatory.'

He poured himself some more wine. May's hand was poised above her apple; Oliver had ceased eating and was gently swirling the whisky in his glass.

'So,' said Rupert, encouraged by their silence, 'that really only leaves the question of where you should sleep, May.'

'Yes, dear?'

'That shouldn't be too much of a problem – there's still the daybed in the studio, isn't there?'

'Are you suggesting,' said Oliver with studied politeness but without looking up, 'that my studio should be turned into a bedroom for May?'

'Not necessarily. The daybed could always be moved in here. We could make it very cosy.'

'Your idea is,' May said, 'that I should live downstairs and Oliver upstairs?'

'Only at night.' He glanced from one to the other, but neither met his eyes. Oliver's calm was an almost palpable force. 'You'd be together during the day – just as you always are.'

'No, dear,' May said, decisively slicing the apple, 'that wouldn't do at all. Supposing Oliver had one of his days in bed and Vi wasn't here, how would I get food up to him – or anything else?'

'That's a difficulty, but I'm sure it could be overcome. Wouldn't one of the neighbours lend a hand? Hazel Maybury –'

'I can't keep calling on Hazel for every blessed thing. We have to be able to manage on our own, you know. Besides, poor Hazel is quite often *hors de combat* and –'

'May.' Oliver lifted his head and spoke firmly. 'May, I have given it a great deal of thought – and I've decided the only sensible thing to do is to have a stairlift installed as soon as possible. Not only will it save your legs, but I shall find it extremely useful myself.' He stared at Rupert. 'Climbing the stairs is an exhausting business for me too, you know.'

'I'm sure it is.'

'I shall sell my Beaverbrook shares. They're a thoroughly third-rate organization these days.'

'I knew you'd find a solution, dear.'

'It's the only sensible thing to do,' he said judicially, picking up his knife and fork and attacking the remains of the steak.

May said, 'I'm afraid the meat is rather on the tough side, isn't it?'

'Not at all, my dear, not at all.' Oliver chewed manfully. 'Very toothsome. How's the Beaune, Rupert?'

'Good – first-class, in fact.'

'Pour a drop into my water glass. No no, just a drop. Yes, that's right. Ummm.' He savoured the wine. 'Quite satisfactory. Can't get anything like this from the Wine Society these days. Do you know they've started purveying the stuff in boxes? *Boxes* – I ask you! I'd sooner drink the prime minister's piss. And where are you off to, my dear?'

May had unhooked her stick from the back of the chair and was struggling to rise. 'To answer a call of nature, if you must enquire.'

Rupert started to get up. 'Can I . . . ?'

But she shook her head, grimly mute. She steadied herself with a hand on Oliver's chair, took a breath, then hobbled painfully to the door.

Father and son looked at each other in silence for a moment.

'I know, I know,' said Oliver, 'but she insists on doing it herself. It's no earthly good offering her a hand. Vi's been longing to wheel her out into the Park all winter, but she won't have it – she seems to have taken a scunner against the wheelchair.' He held out his wine glass. 'Give me a drop more of the Beaune, my lad. That's it, that'll do.'

He ate the last of his steak and took a large mouthful of wine to wash it down.

'It really isn't as tender as it might be, is it?' Rupert said.

'Tough as old boots.'

'I should have pounded it.'

'It's not your fault. It's Vi, I'm afraid – she's almost as bad at buying the food as she is at cooking it.' He cleaned his plate with a piece of bread. 'The truth is, Rupert, ever since your mother gave up on the kitchen, I simply haven't been getting enough to eat.'

'But surely Vi could make you more if you asked?'

'My dear boy, have you ever heard anyone in their right mind asking for more bad food?'

Rupert laughed and refilled their glasses, without demur from the old man. 'Oliver – have you ever considered writing your autobiography?'

'Why? I had a miserable childhood and a lamentable youth – and an extremely trying early manhood. I'd rather forget all about it. Old age is depressing enough as it is without raking up ancient unhappinesses.'

'Then you could miss out the early parts – concentrate on your work.'

'What is this?' Oliver eyed him suspiciously. 'Has May put you up to this? Something to keep me busy now that the Pyramid's finished?'

'Finished! Good heavens – you didn't tell me!'

'Didn't I? Well, I've told you now.' He pursed his lips.

'Look here, of course May didn't put me up to anything. I don't believe she knows – did you tell her?'

'I've mentioned it in passing, but I'm not sure she really took it in.' He blew out his cheeks. 'To tell you the truth, I'd rather have it sink in gradually. She probably feels I'd be even more cantankerous than usual with nothing to keep me occupied – and I expect she's right. Almost anything makes me cantankerous nowadays.'

'But all the same – Oliver, you must be cock-a-hoop.'

'At my age one never feels cock-a-hoop,' he said mournfully. 'Only slightly less awful. Finishing a long project is rather like the aftermath of sexual intercourse, you know. One wonders what all the fuss was about.'

Rupert laughed. 'There's always a next time.'

'Not for me.' He shook his head, but his doleful look gave way to a shy, pleased smile at Rupert's mirth. 'Finish up the wine, my boy. And there's a decanter of port there on the sideboard – you'll want some cheese.'

Rupert took out his cigarettes. 'Would it bother you if I smoked?'

'Not in the least – I can still relish the scent of tobacco. I shall be going to bed soon, I've had a long day – I was up at six. You'll remember about the locking up – and turn out all the lights, I can't rely on May to do that anymore. And if you bank up the fire, with any luck it should stay in all night. And by the way, the glasses should be washed and dried separately – and *not* in soapy water.'

'Right. Locks, lights, fire, glasses. Consider it done.'

'I suppose you think I'm a fussy old fool. I am – but time has a nasty habit of . . . hello?'

The door opened slowly as though pushed by a spectral breeze. May advanced step by step into the room. Under her arm was the cheese board and in her free hand she clutched a muslin-wrapped lump.

'Ah, hello, my dear,' Oliver said heartily. 'All serene?'

'I've brought you the cheddar.'

'How very thoughtful of you, my angel. Cheddar – what could be better?'

'He's in good form, isn't he?'

May popped a morsel of apple into her mouth. 'He's always at his best in company – he needs an audience. I'm afraid I don't provide the required applause.'

They could hear him thumping up the stairs. He was singing as loudly as his cracked old tenor would allow:

> Keep young and beautiful
> It's your duty to be beautiful.
> Keep young and beautiful,
> *If* you want to be . . .

Rupert swallowed some port. The heat of the gas fire had finally swallowed the chill of disuse in the air and brought out the remembered scent of apples and wax and nappery – more remembered than real perhaps. He had noticed dust of neglect, the damp, the tattiness of the old ox-blood velvet curtains as he had closed them against the night. But seen through half-shut eyes the room was much as it had always been – ugly, solid, comforting. He tilted back on his chair.

'I had a letter from Sylvia yesterday morning,' said May.

'Oh hell – did you?' The legs of his chair came down with a bang. 'I was afraid she might do that. What did she say?'

'I think that's rather between her and me, but I am sure you can guess the gist of it.'

'Can't I just!' He couldn't quite keep the bitterness from his voice. 'So now you know. I'd wanted to tell you myself.'

'You don't have to talk to me about it, my dear. I am sure you have your own good reasons.'

'Are you? *I'm* not so sure.' He lit a new cigarette. 'I mean, sure that my reasons are so good. All I know is that I couldn't – couldn't manage it anymore.'

'No, dear. I'm sure we all feel like that at times.'

'Oh.' He stood up and fetched the decanter of port from the sideboard and refilled his glass. 'I still love her, you know,' he said, catching himself in the reflex words of automatic guilt.

'Yes, dear. But too much reliance on love can be quite destructive at times, don't you think?'

Rupert sat down. 'I've never thought that, no – rather the opposite.' He watched her slice another piece of apple – the rings on her time-splotched hand shone as good as new: diamonds from her grandmother, emerald for engagement, gold for wedlock. 'And look where it's got you!' she might have said – but didn't.

'Well, I can tell you – it can be a dreadful burden. Especially for the members of my sex. Apart from making a comfortable, happy home and child-bearing, we don't have a great deal to offer in return. Sometimes it requires a strong sense of duty and loyalty just to carry on.'

'Sylvia's been loyal enough, it's just that . . . .' Quasi-loyal – there'd been that ghastly old fellow Trenchard and Marcel, a beady-eyed little intellectual, others perhaps. But nothing like Trudi, who'd made no bones about sleeping with his friends – and his enemies too, until the distinction between the two had blurred hopelessly. He swallowed the contents of his glass. 'I don't think I've been a bad husband on the whole,' he said lamely.

'I am quite sure you haven't. One's far from believing everything one's told. But –'

'But you disapprove.'

'What an old lady like me thinks is of very little importance. I am sure *you* have thought of the consequences.'

He nodded. 'Sylvia will be alright, it that's what you mean. Better off really. Nowadays she earns more than I do – did. We're going to split the house, and that'll give her quite enough to find a decent place of her own. . . .'

'And what about you, my dear. Have you really resigned from the school?'

'She told you that too, did she? It's true, yes. It could have been quite awkward in the middle of the school year, but as it turns out, they had a replacement up their sleeve and were quite glad to see me go. I suppose I was never really much of a hit as a schoolmaster – always rather on the wrong wavelength, if you know what I mean.'

'And have you considered how it will affect Miranda?'

'Oh, she'll be alright.' He stopped – everyone was going to be 'alright' – everything in the garden was roses. 'Milly doesn't come home very often these days, you see – a few days at Christmas, Easter, a week in the summer, though she doesn't much like Brighton in the summer . . . no, Milly has her own life really.'

'In that case, I don't think we need say anything more about it, do we?' She paused, considering. 'I shan't mention it to your father just yet – he's going to have rather a lot on his plate this weekend.'

'Is he?' Rupert looked at her blankly. 'Oh, yes of course – the hospital. When are you planning to break the news to him?'

'I shall have to discuss that with Miranda – some time over the weekend. It's important to catch him in the right mood.'

'Well, anything I can do to help. . . .'

She smiled at him. 'Your just being there will be a help, my dear.'

'Will it?' Rupert got up and went over to the fire. He was cold. He bent down and warmed his hands. 'It was a bit touch and go there with the stairlift, I thought.' He gave a little laugh.

'Oh, I don't think so. Your father is always quite generous about the important things, you know.'

'But not so hot on the minor expenses?'

'He doesn't really understand about inflation or the cost of living going up – he only reads the obituaries in *The Times*, you know, and that dreadful Bernard Levin. The housekeeping he gives me is exactly the same as it was ten years ago.'

'Ten years – but how on earth do you cope?'

'I eke things out with my pension and every now and again I sell a few of my Premium Bonds. I manage – though I'd be ashamed to tell you how much I pay Vi.'

'But, May, can't you explain to him that –'

'No. I refuse to nag. I never have and I'm not about to begin now. The poor old thing worries about money the whole time as it is.'

'No hope of getting a TV set out of him then?'

'That's quite out of the question.'

'Supposing I was to have a shot at –'

'It's not just a matter of money – he wouldn't stand for it at any price. You know how much he hates me even listening to the wireless.'

'But you used to have television once.'

'That was twenty years ago, when he was out of the house most of the day. He never minded me watching when he wasn't there.'

Rupert smiled; he knew when he was defeated. 'Do you remember the time when we were here one Sunday and Milly pushed it over – the TV set, I mean? She couldn't have been more than three or four at the time – so that must be twenty years ago.'

'I remember very well.'

'And how horrified she was? It was the first really naughty thing she'd ever done. We were watching the racing, as I recall, and she was frightened by the horses. Sylvia put her on bread and milk for half the week.'

'That doesn't surprise me – sadistic and sentimental is what I thought of her as a mother.'

'You . . . .' He looked at her in amazement.

'As a matter of fact, that was the last time we had television in this house. Oliver didn't think it was worth having it repaired.'

'Oh Good Lord – you mean it was our fault?'

'Don't bother yourself about that. I expect he'd have kicked it in himself one fine day.'

Rupert grinned, then chuckled, then laughed outright.

'I don't know why you laugh.'

'Oh May – May!'

She regarded him with a look of enquiry, then shook her head. 'Well, I think I shall bid you goodnight. Perhaps you'd be so good as to bring me up my bag and my library book from the sitting room.'

She took his arm for the slow progress across the hall, but at the foot of the stairs she freed herself and, with one hand on the banister and the other on her stick, hoisted herself onto the first step.

Rupert turned away.

He took up her book and bag, cleared away, did the washing up, but even after he'd dried and put away the last glass, it was still not ten o'clock.

He quickly wrote a few lines to Milly on May's notepaper, put it in an envelope and pinned it to the front door. 'Gone to pub. Back by eleven. Keys on cloakroom windowsill. Love, P.'

Already the clouds were shredding; a few stars shone, the night was fine.

Rupert had never enjoyed pubs, but in the last couple of years he'd got in the habit of popping out for an hour or two every evening – and sometimes he thought the Old Tiger's Head had saved his sanity.

But the Prince Albert was different. The men wore ties and tweed jackets and called each other 'old boy' and drank pints of lager, and the women had perms and white shoes and giggled and drank gin. Not an honest homosexual in sight. It was stepping back into the past.

Rupert was sipping his second large Grouse when he was tapped on the shoulder.

'I am right – it is young Robert, isn't it?'

'Rupert.'

'Rupert – of course. I don't suppose you remember who I am, do you?'

'Of course I do. It's Mr Maybury.'

'Geoffrey, please, Geoffrey.' He smiled warmly. 'How clever of you to recognize me. People often tell me I have a forgettable face, you know – that's what comes of having been in the civil service.' A little spittle flew from his buck teeth as he spoke – the teeth alone would have made him unforgettable. 'And how are your good people?'

'Well, I think – much the same.'

'He is no better. He is much the same, eh? I suppose that goes for us all these days. One crumbles bit by bit at the edges, but one hardly notices it. And then one day . . . .' He nodded his vigorous shock of grey hair. Maybury must have been at least seventy-five, Rupert thought, yet he still possessed a kind of brisk muscularity only betrayed by the large, brown, slightly hangdog eyes. '. . . Phhht!'

'And how's Hazel?'

'Hazel's a bit under the weather this evening, if you know what I mean. A bit under the weather. Not often I get a chance to get out at night, you know. What are you drinking?'

Maybury was drinking Grouse too. When he came back he said, 'I made them triples, I hope you don't mind – it saves having to barge through the crowd all the time. Cheers. And I can't say I care very much for all these people in here, do you?'

'I don't think I know anyone.'

'That's what I mean.'

Later, he said, 'Thank God, I've never had to worry about *that*. Hazel has always had the stuff by the sackful, you see. Of course, she's mean. All rich people are mean, don't you think? Do you know what I had for supper tonight? Sardines on toast – and not even butter under 'em. Margarine. But I let her down, you see. Never got my K. All set for it – thought of herself as Lady Maybury, even started calling herself it to one or two people, most embarrassing. I put up a black mark somehow – was sent off to Trade and Industry. They always shuffle you off to T & I when you're not quite up to snuff, you know. I suppose that's what's wrong with this country in a way.'

'Really?' said Rupert. He'd paid for another round with one of his crisp ten pound notes and was delighted not to have to think.

'I got a good degree – only just missed being a Wrangler, but they were a brilliant lot that year, brilliant. And I'd have had my blue too if I hadn't developed chicken pox three days before the Boat Race. It was always like that with me – odd. I didn't do too badly in the War – wangled myself into the Marines. I was recommended for a DSO, you know, but somehow I only wound up with a mention. I must be boring you a great deal. . . .'

'Far from it.' He lit the last cigarette in the packet, but he'd got twenty more from the machine.

'You were in the war yourself, of course, so –'

'No, I just missed it by two weeks.'

'But didn't you write a book about it?'

'Not about the war, more about the aftermath.'

'Well, I expect that was pretty trying too.'

'It was supposed to be amusing, actually.'

'Yes yes, of course. How silly of me. I remember it now – most enjoyable. So you're a success, aren't you? A famous book under your belt – and I always enjoy those little squibs of yours in *Punch*. And your dear mother tells me of your doings – hither and yon about the world.'

'I've spent the last fifteen years in Brighton.'

'Have you? I'm very fond of Brighton. Haven't been there for – oh – fifty years, I suppose. Hazel dislikes the sea, you see – she's a mountain girl. We went to Pontresina every Whitsun and the Lake District in the summer of course. She wants her ashes scattered in the Enghadien – that worries me rather. I mean, how does one scatter ashes? Perhaps I should hire a helicopter, what do you think?'

'How about a hang-glider? They're always hang-gliding off the top of Mont Blanc.'

'Ah, but the Mont Blanc isn't in the Enghadien. You see – it's not so simple.'

'It's a problem. Would you care for a drink? I think they want to close up?'

'How very kind of you, yes. You know,' he said, with a generous spray of spittle, new glass in hand, 'the funny thing is, the older I grow, the less and less I seem to be able to understand women – or anyone else for that matter.'

'Well, of course, they *are* the opposite sex.'

'I hadn't thought of that one.' He laughed. 'By Jove – you're right. The opposite sex. Explains a lot, eh? I mean, why they're always so confoundedly critical, do y'know?'

'Do you read much poetry?'

'Not nowadays, my dear fellow. I used to be very fond of Browning when I was an undergraduate. I did read a poem in the *Observer* the other day – all about the hindquarters of a cow. Not my cup of tea.'

'Ever read any John Crowe Ransom?'

'Can't say I have, no – why? Not a cow pat chap, I hope.'

'No no – what you said about women. He has a line or two. . . .' Rupert braced himself, the Scotch could easily mess up the esses if he wasn't careful. '. . . Cold worse – words, I mean. Cold words came down spiral from the head, Grey doves from the officious tower ill-sped.'

'The officious tower – ill-sped? I say, I like that. I like that very much. How does it go on?'

'It's longish – can't remember it all.'

'Nothing?'

'Oh yes – wait a minute, here's a bit.' He took a deep breath of smoke and spirit fumes and raised his voice against the late pub babble. 'Great lovers,' he intoned, 'lie in Hell, the stubborn ones, Infatuate of the flesh upon the bones; Stuprate, they –'

'What's that?'

'Stuprate!' Rupert roared as the heads began to turn, 'Stuprate, they rend each other when they kiss. The pieces kiss again – no end to this.'

One or two people laughed; somebody began to clap.

'Splendid,' said Maybury, 'absolutely splendid!'

On the other side of London, in Kentish Town, a half-naked young man lay on an unmade bed or couch.

'Come on,' he said, 'stop mousing around, come back here.'

'Isn't there *any*thing to eat in this rathole?'

'What do you care about fucking food?'

'I'm bloody starving – I haven't had anything all day except a bun at the station.'

'There's a can of baked beans in the fridge.' He started to roll a cigarette.

'There isn't. I looked.'

'In the freezer part, ducky.'

'In the freezer? God, you're mad as well as disgusting. Frozen baked beans!'

'The fridge is on the blink, didn't you notice?' He put out his tongue and slowly moistened the cigarette paper. 'Come on, Andy – forget the fucking beans, get your tight little ass over here.'

'Who do you think you are with that fake American accent – JR?'

'Who's JR?'

'A guy who's just about as nasty as you, but a lot cleaner. Don't you ever have a bath?'

'The shower's kaput.' He lit the cigarette and flicked away a few burning shreds of tobacco.

'Well, take one at the hospital once in a while.'

'We're on strike, as if you didn't know.'

'Against soap? Or just the general public?'

'Screw the public. Come here, Andy, and let's fuck.'

'I wish you'd stop this "Andy" business – why can't you call me Milly like everyone else?'

'I'm not like everyone else – Andy.'

'That's true. *Andy* – why that? I think you must be a latent gay.'

'Them's fighting words.'

'Come on, everyone knows you were at Harrow – all public schoolboys are basically homosexual.'

'Harrow!' he shouted, touched on the raw.

'Well wherever it was, you're probably a repressed cock-sucker.'

'Floreat,' he sang at the top of his voice, 'Floreat, floreat Rugbeia, Floreat, floreat –'

'Floreat buggery.'

'Never!' He sat up abruptly and half the burning tobacco fell out on his chest. 'Never!' he cried, beating at the ashes. 'Nothing more than a quick feel up behind the gym.' He lay back with a grin. 'Very very chaste. Come on, Milly, finish the bloody beans and come here.'

'No, Archie. I'll miss the last train if I do.'

'Fuck the last train! What the hell do you care about your fucking parents? They dropped you in the shit, what –'

'It's not my parents – it's my grandparents.'

'Grandparents! Jesus Christ on a crutch!' He laughed.

'Shut up. I'm very fond of my grandparents – besides they're old and –'

'– and rich? And they live in Esher and he's a J.P. and she's a –'

'East Sheen. And he isn't – a J.P., I mean – but she was, I think.'

'Listen, forget about the train, I'll take you there in the bus.'

'The bus! I'm not going on a bus.'

'The ambulance, nudnik. It's parked right outside.'

'But you can't do that.'

'Why not? Nobody stops an ambulance. Come on.'

'I'll have to make a phone call.'

'You can't – it's been cut off for weeks.'

'Oh Archie, you bastard.'

'Come here. Milly-mouse. Please.'

'Bastard. You are a bastard.'

2

Saturday

Rupert came awake slowly and lay staring at the ceiling without the least idea of where he was. His mouth was dry and woolly, his back ached – he'd been bent over sweeping a flight of old stone steps with a carving knife. And there was singing, as if from a chapel or chantry; and then the words came clear and the threads of the dream slipped away.

> In the good old summer time,
> In the good old summer time,
> We'll go walking down the shady lane
> In the good old . . .

It was Oliver singing somewhere close by.

Rupert rolled his legs off the couch and sat up. He was vaguely surprised to find himself fully clothed. He stood up with an effort and went over to the window and pulled back the curtain. The sunlight struck him between the eyes and he stepped back with a grunt and, reaching out blindly for support, caught hold of the longcase clock which tottered and jangled.

'Blast,' he said, steadying it with both hands – but it had suffered no damage and beat on plaintively in its usual way. And from the kitchen came the harsh whirr of an electric coffee grinder. His head ached and his body felt heavy as though, like the clock, laden with lead weights. He rubbed the stiff hairs on his chin. It was a very long time since he'd been drunk.

'Good morning,' he said, entering the kitchen, 'glorious morning.'

Oliver stopped the coffee grinder. He was dressed in striped pyjamas and a large brown dressing gown. The sunlight shone through the thin remnants of his hair making a soft silver halo. 'What?' he said crossly.

'Lovely morning.'

'Is it?' He pressed down firmly on the grinder.

Rupert went to the Easiwork and switched on the old bakelite radio. There was a sudden loud contralto blast.

'What's that bloody row?' Oliver shouted.

'Sorry.' Rupert turned it down. 'The Queen of Night, isn't it?'

Oliver ceased grinding. 'The *Queen*?'

'The Queen of Night – *The Magic Flute*, you know.'

'Oh her.' He poured the grounds into the aluminium basket of the coffee pot. 'Yawping bitch.'

Rupert changed stations. '. . . yesterday voted for a series of one-day strikes and slowdowns aimed at disrupting commuter traffic at selected . . .' He switched it off.

'Bloody barbarians!' Oliver carefully tapped the basket to level off the coffee, then bore the pot over to the stove and set it on the gas. 'Do you want coffee?'

'No thanks. I'll make some tea.'

'Tea – filthy muck.' He went back to the table and sat down and watched Rupert filling the kettle. 'You're dressed. You must have been up early. I didn't hear you.'

'As a matter of fact, I slept on the couch in the sitting room.' He put a light under the kettle.

'What in God's name for?'

'I was waiting up for Milly.'

'Oh, Miranda. How is she?'

'She hasn't come in yet.'

'Hasn't come in? Good God.' He blinked rapidly. 'Didn't she ring?'

'Not yet – I don't suppose she'd want to wake us up this early.'

'It's gone nine.' The old man's shoulders drooped. 'Where could she be?'

'She probably missed the last train and had to stop over night,' Rupert said, forcing a cheerful tone. 'I'd hardly expect her to come home with the milk.'

'The milkman doesn't come till ten on Saturdays,' Oliver said lugubriously. 'Stop with whom?'

'One of her friends, I imagine.'

'Oh. The lame duck?'

'Well – er, yes. One of them.'

'I thought disabled birds were generally shot, not coddled,' he said dryly.

'Aren't you thinking of horses?'

'I doubt it. I very seldom think of horses – although I do know the difference between a duck and a dog.'

'I expect you do.' Rupert smiled, puzzled. 'I mean, why shouldn't you?'

'Turn it down, will you? The coffee, man – can't you hear it bubbling? As low as it will go.'

Rupert lowered the gas and the sudden fresh scent of coffee overpowered the staleness of old meals badly cooked, the traces of which stained the walls and lay greasy on the flat surfaces. The kitchen looked irretrievably shabby in the morning sun.

'The herons never came back after the war, you know,' Oliver said meditatively.

'Didn't they? I didn't know, no.' He rinsed the teapot – it had a film of old tea with mould at the bottom. 'What herons?'

'The herons in the Park. The ack-ack batteries frightened them off in the Blitz and they stopped nesting in Sidmouth Wood. They never came back.'

'What a shame.' He thought of his own kitchen in Brighton, spick and span, neat as a new pin, with the seagulls crying and cawing in the morning – a noise Sylvia detested, as she detested the sea and the cold winter winds cutting up the lanes, which he relished. How had it come to pass that all the things he loved, she loathed? One by one the qualities he cherished in her had been drawn like individual pebbles from the beach and sucked away into the sea's general rant.

'Sorry – what did you say?'

'I said – how did you sleep on the couch?'

'Alright – fine.'

'Didn't you hear the dog?'

'What dog?'

'The Hamiltons' dog. It barked all night. I hardly slept a wink. They let it run in the garden – in heat, I should think, whining and yelping and tearing up the flower beds. Ought to be shot.'

'Oh now – you can't shoot a dog just because it's in heat.'

'I wasn't talking about the dog. I meant the Hamiltons. The coffee's ready now – bring over the pot, would you?' He poured himself a cup. 'Of course, she is a foreigner.'

'Who is?'

'Mrs Hamilton.'

'Have you got anything against foreigners?'

'Only *en masse*. I was extremely fond of that first wife of yours – what was her name?'

'Trudi. That's because she made up to you.'

'Made up to me?'

'Flirted with you.'

'Nonsense. At my age?'

'That never troubled Trudi – she slept with blokes a good deal older than you were then.'

'My dear boy – you never told me!' He stared at Rupert in innocent amazement, then took a sip of coffee. 'How dreadful for you. This is extremely good coffee, by the way – are you sure you won't change your mind and have a cup? You look as though you could do with it.'

'Do I?' Rupert smiled. 'But no thanks – my tea's ready now.'

'Frankly, you look like the wrath of God – but then I expect I do myself with my hair all over the place like this. Mr Mason hasn't been able to come for almost a month – broke a big toe falling out of his car, poor chap – but the net result is I feel untidy the whole time.'

'I could do with a haircut myself.' Rupert carried his cup of tea to the kitchen table and took a stool opposite his father. He lit a cigarette and they sat in companionable silence – the smoke curling in the sunlight and flattening out into thin layers.

Oliver said suddenly. 'I'm extremely worried about Miranda.'

'I don't think you need be – she can look after herself alright.'

'You may not realize it in Islay, but London is a very dangerous place indeed these days.'

Rupert laughed. 'I don't live in Islay, you know.'

'I am perfectly well aware of that – it was merely a figure of speech denoting otherworldliness.'

'Brighton's fairly dangerous too.'

'But she's not *in* Brighton, is she? And the fact is you haven't the faintest idea *where* she is, have you?'

'No – but she's bound to turn up sooner or later.'

'No doubt – in the Thames.'

'That's a bit morbid, isn't it?'

'What if she doesn't *turn up*?'

Frowning, Rupert tipped some ash into his saucer. 'Milly may be a little offhand about some of the minor details of life, but she's totally reliable about the important things.'

'I admire your forbearance, Rupert.' He drained his cup. 'All I can say is – if you had ever expected me to sit up all night fully clothed waiting for you and then turned up in the morning to tell me it was a minor detail, I should have had one or two pretty powerful things to say to you.'

'But I never did, did I?'

'No, although I don't mind saying you gave me one or two anxious moments – particularly about your religion.'

Rupert laughed.

'I'm glad you are able to see the humour of the situation.' He drained his cup and stood up. 'I, I may say, am desperately worried.'

'Lord save us,' Rupert murmured under his breath.

'I'm going upstairs to get dressed,' Oliver announced, tightening the cord of his dressing gown. 'I can't face a crisis in pyjamas.'

'Oh quite. Do you think May would care for a cup of tea?'

'Your mother makes her own tea in the morning.' He paused at the doorway. 'Incidentally, she didn't have at all a good night either.'

Rupert stubbed out his cigarette and poured himself another cup of tea.

Going up the stairs, the old man was singing – a different air this time:

> Oh do not grieve me,
> Oh never leave me –
> How could you use a poor maiden so?

Where the devil *was* Milly?

May backed against the door to close it – and rested there a minute. Her shoulders hunched, she seemed smaller than usual; her skin was greyish and her cheeks had none of their old-lady bloom. She had her stick in her left hand and in her right she carried a bowl with a small jug of milk in it. As she crept painfully to her chair, her hand shook and the jug rattled against the bowl. She put them on the table and lowered herself with extreme care, but, all the same, dropped the last few inches with a jerk that made her wince. For quite a long time she sat with her eyes shut, still as death.

The striking of the clock roused her at last. She hooked the footstool with her stick and pulled it over and put her feet on it. She drew the shawl from the back of the chair, spread it over her lap, and put on her glasses. Taking up each bottle in turn, she shook out her pills and then made several notations in a small exercise book. She poured a glass of water, sniffed it, nodded, and swallowed the pills one by one with a quick jerk of her head.

She had begun to mix the bran and the milk in the bowl when the phone rang. It took her quite a long time to put down the bowl and pick up the receiver, which almost slipped out of her fingers.

'Seven-five-four three . . . oh, it's you, Vi. Oh, so-so. No, not very good. You could? But what about your husband? I see. Oh Vi – that would be a relief. . . .' Her voice wavered, then she got control of it. 'And if it wouldn't be too much trouble, perhaps you could bring up a cauliflower and a couple of extra pounds of potatoes. . . .'

On the other side of the road a high brick wall bounded the Park and, beyond it, the tops of a stand of oaks stood bare-branched against the brilliant spring sky. A troop of small children on large horses lolloped by. Leaning over the gate, Rupert waved, and a girl in pigtails gravely nodded acknowledgement.

He cleared his throat as a middle-aged woman with a corgi marched past but, head held high, she made no sign of having seen him. Not a neighbour then – or perhaps simply not neighbourly. In the old days, Oliver had been in the habit of shouting at neighbours for the most trivial of offences – and dog ladies were a particular *bête noire*. There had been one – Miss Tree-Ponting – whose dachshund had repeatedly bitten Rupert without provocation (each incident requiring a quick visit to Dr Goodman to cauterize the wound at seven and sixpence a time). Then one Saturday morning, the dog had made the mistake of attacking him when in company with Oliver, who had stepped forward smartly and with one well-directed kick had lifted the animal in the air and clear across the road into a laurel bush. 'Oh you wicked man!' had cried the lady and for one glorious moment, Rupert had thought Oliver was going to kick her too.

'Excuse me – do you think Mrs Darley is at home?'

Rupert straightened up. 'Yes of course – won't you come in?'

'Oh no – I would not wish to disturb her. I am Mrs Hamilton from next door and I –'

'I'm Rupert Darley – the son, you know. How-do-you-do?' He held out his hand.

Mrs Hamilton was small, dark-haired and pretty – and should have been svelte, but there was a nervousness about her manner as she awkwardly disentangled her hand from a large bunch of

flowers she was holding. Her palm was slightly damp.
'Do come in,' said Rupert, smiling.
'No no, please. I wanted just to apologize about Elsa and –'
'Elsa? Your dog?'
'You heard her! Oh dear, she was awful last night and I am so afraid that –'
'Didn't hear a thing,' Rupert reassured her.
'You didn't. Oh.' She was nonplussed.
'As a matter of fact I had a few too many last night – went out like a light. I doubt whether I'd have heard the Hound of the Baskervilles if he'd chanced to be cavorting about East Sheen.' He saw that she'd not understood a word. 'Drunk,' he said, '*betrunken – soũl.*'
'Oh.' She looked at him squarely for the first time and there was a flicker of a smile at the corners of her mouth.
'What sort of a dog is she?'
'An Irish setter. Are you fond of dogs?'
'Not much – are you?'
'To say the truth, I do not like them either – and my little girl is frightened of Elsa, but my husband says . . . .' She tailed off.
'That all decent English families should have a dog?'
'Something like that.' She gave him a shy, but real smile this time. 'But your parents,' she said, serious again, 'I am sure they were wakened. So will you please give these to Mrs Darley and say how sorry we are for all the noise and we will try to see that it does not happen again.' And she handed him the huge cellophane-wrapped bundle of flowers and nodded and started to turn away.
'I say.'
'Yes?' She stopped.
'Are you going round giving bouquets to everyone, if it isn't a rude question?'
'Oh no. Our neighbours on the other side are not at all nice.' And she gave a little laugh that showed her teeth.
As he watched her walk away with small crisp steps, a voice behind him said, 'Charming little lady.'

Rupert turned. 'Oh, good morning, Geoffrey – yes, isn't she?'

'Hamilton must have something the rest of us don't know about. He's a terrible stick – a diplomat, of course.'

'Of course.' Rupert grinned.

'Sent her round with flowers, did he? The wretched dog, I suppose. Won't give us the time of day.'

'Were you kept awake too?'

'Not really, not last night – in the circumstances,' he smiled old-maidishly. 'But it happens two or three times a week.'

'It must cost him a packet at the florist.'

'Must, yes. But there aren't any flowers in their garden, you know – that poor hound has torn everything up by the roots, and it used to be so charming before they moved in. But she's Swiss, you see – and the Swiss are not noted dog-lovers.'

'Fonder of flowers, no doubt.'

'Shouldn't think so. All those glorious meadows full of wild flowers – never see a native set foot in them. Frightened of mountains too. Odd people. Well – give my respects to your good mother.'

Rupert turned smiling from the gate. He wondered what Mrs Hamilton's first name was – she reminded him of someone. He paused to listen – and then ran down the path. In the house the phone was ringing.

'Was that Milly on the phone?'

'No, dear – it was Vi.'

'Oh.' Rupert sat down on the couch and laid the flowers beside him. He was short of breath and his head throbbed.

'She's very kindly offered to come and make the lunch. Her husband has fortunately decided to spend the day with his mother, so Vi's free. She doesn't get on with her mother-in-law – I gather the old lady is rather a Tartar.'

'Oh really?' He wiped the back of his neck with his handkerchief.

May ate a small spoonful of bran. 'No news of Miranda then, I take it?'

'No, not yet. But she'll be along.'

'Of course she will.'

'Oh by the way, these are for you. From Mrs Hamilton – a sort of peace offering for the noise the dog made last night.'

'That blessed dog! Well, come on, let's have a look. Oh dear – gladioli and tiger lilies – how very funereal.'

'I'll put them in water,' he said, not moving.

'I suppose you'd better, dear. A kind thought. But then she's a very kind little lady. They were a bit standoffish at first, but then when he discovered that Oliver had built the embassy in – well, I can't remember the country, but somewhere where Mr Hamilton had served – then they were all over us. They sent us a brace of grouse and at Christmas presented us with a whole smoked ham and Mrs Hamilton is always running in with pots of honey and country butter – and once, when she'd heard Oliver say how much he liked it, she made him a whole jugged hare and brought it in and served it up to us one Saturday night. Of course now she can do no wrong in his eyes.'

'Oh I don't know, he was talking about having her shot this morning,' he said – and then immediately regretted it.

May gave a tired sigh and closed her eyes for a long moment.

'I expect he meant the dog,' said Rupert quickly.

'What that poor animal needs is a good brisk five-mile walk two or three times a day.'

'Or a cold bath,' Rupert murmured feelingly. Having neglected to turn on the immersion heater, he'd shaved and bathed in somewhat less than tepid water. 'Were you much disturbed? Oliver said you had a baddish night.'

'It was the pain, my dear, not the dog.'

'But what about your painkillers?'

'I took two, but then I woke up again at five in absolute agony – so I remembered what you said and took two more.'

'I said? What did I say?'

'You said I should ignore what it said on the bottle about only taking six every twenty-four hours.'

'Oh. Well – that's what painkillers are for, aren't they? There's no virtue in being stoical about pain when you can simply take a pill and stop it.'

'No,' she said bleakly, '–although I used to think there was. But it seems to me I never knew what pain was – day in, day out. It's horrid – it makes you cross and sulky and sorry for yourself – all the things I've always despised . . . I used to think Oliver made a ridiculous fuss and bother about all his aches and pains and his heart attacks – but now I think I was rather unfeeling.'

'But you're not like that, May.'

'Oh but I am, my dear, I am – though I try not to show it. I have to bite my tongue twenty times a day.' She smoothed the shawl over her knees.

'It's like old age itself, you see,' she went on wearily. 'You assume you know all about it – after all, we've all watched elderly relatives pottering about, knitting and nodding. I never thought anything much of it. In fact I remember on my sixtieth birthday running upstairs and stopping on the landing and looking out at the Judas tree in bloom and thinking, "Now I'm an old lady" – but I felt exactly the same as I had at forty. What's all the fuss about? I thought. But that was twenty-five years ago – and now I know.'

'Twenty-five years. . . .' Rupert got up and stood in front of the fire. He opened an inlaid ebony box on the mantelpiece; it was filled with teeth – baby teeth, milk teeth, the long fangs of wisdom teeth. 'And I was just getting married,' he murmured.

'And which wife was that, dear?'

Rupert looked at her, startled – was her memory getting as bad as that? And then he smiled. 'Number two – Sylvia,' he said and gently closed the lid of the box.

'How very nice for you, dear.'

He laughed. 'Well, I'd better see to those glads.'

'You'll find a suitable vase in the landing cupboard – the tall, rather heavy one you used to make ice in when you were a little boy.'

'Ice?' he said, 'did I?' But he was thinking of Mrs Hamilton. He knew now whom she had reminded him of – Trudi, wife number one.

'Hello, Vi,' he said, taking the last steps carefully – filled with water, the vase was unconscionably heavy and the flowers obscured his view of his feet.

'Hello, Mister Rupert. Can I give you a hand?'

'No thanks. There we are.' He rested the vase on the hallstand. 'How are you then?'

'I'm very well, thank you – except for my shingles, but they're getting better now.' Vi was a large woman who looked as though she had been pumped up with a bicycle pump – and her fatness was of the billowy kind that seemed to carry her along rather than weigh her down.

'Oh bad luck. I had shingles once – most unpleasant.'

'Unpleasant. The doctor's given me a sort of spray thing and that makes it ever so much better.'

'Oh good – splendid.' He noticed she too was carrying flowers – daffodils. 'And your husband – he's alright?'

'Henry's very well, thank you.' Her voice had an odd lilting, yet at the same time toneless quality. There seemed to be no connection between the rhythm of her words and their sense – she could just as easily have been saying, 'Henry's dying of lead poisoning, thank you.'

'Well, that's fine,' said Rupert, 'fine.'

'Fine. And how's Mrs Darley this morning?'

'Not so well, I'm afraid – she had a bad night.'

'One of her bad nights, yes. Well, I'll just pop in then.'

'Right.' He opened the door and hoisted the vase and preceded her into the sitting room.

'Good morning, Madam. I've brought you some daffodils.'

'How very kind of you, Vi.' May put on her glasses and inspected them. 'Are they from the garden?'

'Garden. Yes, just the last of them – the little boys next door have had most of the rest. Henry's rung up the local police station twice about it. I tell him the police have got better things to do than guard our daffodils, but he won't listen of course.'

Rupert said, 'Where shall I put these, May?'

'On top of the radiogram, I think, dear – they'll be out of the way there. Did you remember the cauliflower, Vi?'

'Yes, I did – and I brought an extra loaf of bread as well as the potatoes – I thought you might be needing it over the weekend.'

'Yes, I expect we shall. Now, for lunch. . . .'

Rupert went to the window and lit a cigarette. He had a vague hope of catching sight of Milly, but the evergreen hedge had grown too thick and high to see what passed in the road. Would she have enough sense to go to Richmond and take a taxi? It really was too bad of her – already it was well after eleven.

'Rupert?'

'Yes? What? – sorry.'

'Vi wants to know if you'd like some coffee.'

'I'm making some for the Master, so it wouldn't be any trouble.'

'Oh – no. No thanks.' Coffee, he thought, filthy muck. What he really needed was a pint of bitter.

'Is there anything I can get you then, Madam? A hot water bottle for your knees?'

'That would be kind.'

'Very well, Madam.'

Vi went out in a kind of mechanical bustle, like a wind-up toy.

Rupert came back to the fire.

'May,' he said, 'about this hospital business. I –'

'Not now, dear, if you don't mind,' she said as a door banged in the hall. 'I think he's coming.'

'Ah, May,' said Oliver, throwing open the door, 'there you are!' He wore a short-sleeved open neck shirt and a yellow jumper and looked quite sporty.

'Where else would I be?'

'Eh?'

'Oughtn't you to be wearing a jacket?'

'I've just looked – it's seventy out and going to go higher.'

'The good old summertime,' said Rupert.

'May, I've just written to the stairlift people, ordering them to proceed at once with measuring us up.' He brandished a letter.

'Terrific!' Rupert said.

'At four thousand pounds, it certainly terrifies me, if that's what you mean. I'm off to the post. If this doesn't catch the midday collection, it won't go till Monday.'

'I'll take it for you, if you like.'

'Would you, my boy?' He looked uncertainly at Rupert. 'That's very kind of you. I won't say no. But you'd better hurry, you've barely got twenty minutes.'

'It's only just up the road.' Rupert took the letter. 'Maybe I'll meet Milly on the way.'

'Hasn't she rung yet?'

'Not yet, but I –'

'Christ Almighty! You'd better call the police at once!'

'I really don't think that's necessary.'

'Well – alright. On your head be it.' He grunted. 'I shall go and read the paper in the summerhouse.'

He walked out without a trace of yesterday's old man's shuffle. As soon as the door closed he started to sing:

> I'm stepping out, my dear,
> To breathe an atmosphere
> That simply reeks of class . . .

Smiling, Rupert looked down at May. Her head was bowed and her hands were cupped over her eyes and she made a small choking sound.

'Why, May!'

'Oh Rupert!' She was sobbing now. 'Do you think something really could have happened to her?'

He knelt down and put his arms round her. 'My dear, my dear – of course nothing's happened to her. She's all right – just a little thoughtless perhaps. But she'll be here for lunch, I promise you.'

'Oh dear oh dear, I am so upset. I don't know why. But he does carry on so. I know I'm just being a silly old lady. . . .'

'There there,' he rocked her gently, 'don't be upset, my love – you needn't be upset. It'll be alright.'

'Do you think so? I do so hope you're right.' She dabbed at her eyes with a small handkerchief.

'I know I'm right.' Rupert sat back on his haunches. 'It's going to be a good day.'

'But I am so dreading it.' She gave a trembling sigh and then, with a kind of wistful vehemence, 'The truth is, Rupert, that I don't want to go on. That's all I want – not to go on anymore. I don't want to have to sit here hour after hour. I don't want him coming in every minute of the day telling me what he's going to do or where he's just been. I don't want to be *badgered*! I've had enough.'

Rupert took her hand. 'He's an awkward old cuss – perhaps if I were to –'

Suddenly she cried out, 'If only he would die and leave me to depart in peace!'

Rupert felt the tears in his own eyes. 'You're tired, my old dear, aren't you – tired of waiting?'

She nodded and closed her eyes and held his hand a little tighter. And they stayed like that as the old clock ticked.

'I've brought your hot-water bottle, Madam.'

Rupert stood up.

'There, I'll just put it under your shawl, shall I?'

'Oh, thank you, Vi dear.'

'And I've brought you a fresh jug of water. I'll bring in the daffodils in a moment – unless you'd prefer them in the bedroom?'

'I'd better be going,' said Rupert, picking up the letter from the floor.

'Yes, dear, you run off.'

'Oh and Vi,' he said, 'you'd better take my father's coffee to him in the summerhouse.'

'Summerhouse. Yes, I will.'

Oliver took a mouthful of coffee – Vi made good coffee, she couldn't be faulted on that – but it wasn't the same without a cigar. A woman is only a woman, but a good cigar. . . .

The birds on the lawn – a few tits and sparrows and a single sleek-headed blackbird – were suddenly disturbed by the advent of a couple of fat pigeons who immediately began to throw their weight about, disputing the breadcrumbs Oliver had scattered.

He got up from the canvas chair and flapped *The Times* at them from the entrance of the summerhouse.

'Go away, you damned fat brutes,' he called, and they all flew up at once and perched in the apple tree.

Oliver returned to the paper – Saturday obituaries were generally on the dull side and there was no one he knew or had even heard of: Eminent Clinical Psychiatrist – he skipped that one; an ancient clergyman ('His Victorian Gothic vicarage was full of the dusty chaos in which he liked to live'); and – ah, much better – a Swindon train driver who'd won the George Cross for single-handedly driving a blazing ammunition train through a tunnel and out into the open country where it had exploded harmlessly, killing a handful of cows.

The sides of the summerhouse were glassed-in and it was bakingly hot inside. Oliver began to close his eyes as the smell of dust mingled with sweat and the acrid odour of gunfire. He crouched in the chalk pit with what was left of his platoon – the ground sloped evenly away from the German machine-gun position on the railway embankment and the intermittent bursts forced their heads down. Despite the intense heat, there was water in the bottom of the pit – impossible to keep one's feet out of it. The sweat trickled down his back and from the brim of his tin hat into his eyes. There was a nasty graze on the knuckles of his hand. There were flies everywhere. He could scarcely breathe in the heat. He gripped his service revolver more tightly. 'Sergeant Davis,' he said, 'I think we'd better make a run for it. . . .'

Run for it . . . run for it. . . . He lifted his head and blinked away the daze of sleep. He took several quick shallow breaths; he reached for the pillbox in the ticket pocket at the top of his trousers – then let his hand fall back. No, he didn't need a pill. Not this time.

The coffee was tepid, but he drank it all the same. The birds had come back to the lawn.

Rupert turned away from the Park gates reluctantly. Like Mrs Hamilton's dog, he could have done with a brisk five-mile walk. His body felt stale and old and his head stupid and thick. He longed for solitude as May longed for release. He too knew what it was to be badgered – the endless schoolboy chatter, the meaningless questions, the Common Room sarcasm, and Sylvia's icy words in the bare evenings. He did not want to go back to Wisteria Cottage – not right away. May's tears bled in him like old wounds, and he wanted to cover them up and retreat.

The postman was scooping the letters out of the mail box into his sack. 'Morning,' he said cheerfully, giving Rupert a quick glance and nod.

'Good morning,' said Rupert heavily.

The man slammed the door of the box, locked it, and hopped into his van. With a scoot of loose gravel, the van sped away down the road. In front of one of the houses there was an ambulance, glistening white in the sunlight. Rupert took a few steps – and then he was running.

It was hardly a hundred yards to Wisteria Cottage, but it seemed like nightmare miles. He was half way there when the ambulance drew abruptly away. As it passed him a hand waved from the cab and the siren gave a single *pam-pam*. Rupert turned his head, stumbled, recovered and ran on, his heart in his mouth.

In the summerhouse the old man woke up with a jerk and *The Times* slid from his knees onto the floor.

'Damn,' he murmured. He cocked his head to catch the sound that had woken him, alert with a sense of danger. But the garden was quiet and only the passing of a plane on its way to Heathrow disturbed the stillness. He retrieved the paper and shoved it under his arm and got up, steadying himself against the doorpost. The birds on the grass stirred a little.

'Make a run for it . . . make a run for it . . .' beat at the back of his mind. But he was muzzy with sunlight and stiff with sleep, and could move only very slowly. The birds parted courteously to let him pass, not bothering to take wing.

At the garden gate, Miranda stood quite still, watching her father gallumphing down the road. She was tall, small-boned, with a whippet-like leanness – no make-up and her dark hair cut short. She wore jeans and a man's collarless shirt and carried a large woven bag over one shoulder, a scarlet raincoat over her arm and a bunch of tulips in her hand.

She wiped her mouth with the back of her hand.

'Milly!' Rupert slowed and stopped.

'Hello, Daddy.'

Rupert held onto the gate post, gasping. 'I thought you'd never get here!'

'Well, here I am.' She smiled, watchful.

He took a step towards her and they kissed awkwardly, and he stepped back.

'Phew,' she said, 'you stink of old whisky and cigarettes. You're smoking again.'

'Five or ten a day. Who was that?'

'Archie. Oh don't say you've forgotten already – I only brought him home at Christmas.'

'Oh yes – the chap who got chucked out of medical school and wouldn't eat turkey. Why the ambulance?'

'Because he's an ambulance driver. It's alright – they're on strike at the moment.'

'I see – so that makes it alright.' And who pays for the petrol, he thought – but kept his peace. 'Is that where you were all night?'

'Yes,' she said, failing to keep out the defiance, 'if it's any business of yours.'

'You can spend every night with the King of Siam as far as I'm concerned,' he said, furious suddenly. 'But you might have had the elementary decency to give us a phone call – we were damnably worried!'

'Were you?' she said coolly, 'well, I'm sorry – but Archie's phone's been cut off.'

They glared at each other – neither of them seeing Oliver slowly rounding the corner of the house. Suddenly Rupert burst out laughing.

Miranda gave a hesitant smile, then laughed softly. 'I *am* sorry, Poopa – I truly am, but –'

'Well, you're safe now.'

'Am I?' She looked at him quizzically. 'And what are you doing here? I didn't know you were coming.'

'I only made up my mind yesterday.' He hesitated. 'You haven't got my letter, I suppose?'

'What –'

'Miranda!' called Oliver, waving the paper as he came up to them. 'Miranda, my dear!'

'Grandad!' She pushed open the gate and ran down to him and put her arms round him and kissed him on both cheeks.

'Well, well,' he said with a shy smile. 'How very nice to see you, my dear.'

'You too. I'm sorry to be so late. But look, I've got something for you,' she said, rummaging in her bag.

'For me?'

'Here,' she said, pulling it free, 'a sponge!'

'Look, May, Miranda's brought me a sponge – all the way from Rhodes. A real Rhodes sponge!'

'Hello, Granny dear,' said Miranda, bending to kiss her. 'And I've brought you something too.' She put a small tissue-wrapped parcel in May's lap. 'Oh – and tulips. I hope you like tulips?'

'That's very kind of you. I'm always pleased to get tulips – so self-possessed they seem, don't they?'

'It smells of the sea,' Oliver said, sniffing at the sponge, 'it smells of Greece!'

'*Thalassa thalassa*,' said Rupert.

'This *is* pretty, my dear.' May held up a small dish with a fish painted on it. 'It will do very nicely for my pins. Thank you.'

'And this is nothing less than munificence.' Oliver plumped down in his chair, still clutching the sponge. 'My old sponge is in rags. Exactly what I needed – it'll last me for years.'

May groaned faintly.

'The plate's from Greece too, isn't it, Milly?' said Rupert.

'Is it?' May looked up. 'I didn't know you'd been to Greece recently.'

'Well – in January. Didn't you get my card?'

'I don't think so – did we, Oliver?'

'Of course we got her card – a rather inferior reconstruction of the Colossus.'

May raised her eyebrows. 'I never liked Greece very much – I always thought it was rather smelly.'

'Lord-love-a-duck,' muttered Oliver.

'*Lovely* and smelly,' Miranda said with a grin, 'roast fish and oil and ouzo. A great improvement on formaldehyde.' She sat down on the couch.

'Is that a nasty smell, dear? I don't think I know what it is.'

'It's what they use to preserve corpses,' said Oliver.

May wrinkled her nose. 'How horrid. I have no wish to be preserved. I just want to be cremated and out of the way as quickly as possible.'

'They wouldn't have the slightest use for our remains, my dear. I should be delighted to give my carcase to science – if I thought science would be remotely interested.'

'It might if you had some rare disease.' Miranda patted the place beside her and Rupert sat down.

'The only disease I suffer from is old age – and garrulity,' Oliver said complacently, 'neither of which are either interesting or rare.'

'I understood you wanted to be burned on a huge pyre like the Hindus,' May said. 'Suttee, I think they call it.'

'Suttee is the practice of immolating a widow on her *husband*'s pyre – of which I do not approve.'

'I should have thought you might have considered that rather a good idea.'

'It wouldn't do Hazel Maybury any harm. But in general I have very little use for the Hindus – nor shall have until they start eating their sacred cows.'

'Well, dear, you have very little use for *humanity* in general.'

'Perfectly true,' Oliver smirked. 'Perfectly true. I admire the Greeks of course – but everything's gone to the dogs since then.'

'Did the Ancient Greeks have handkerchiefs?' asked May sweetly.

Rupert laughed.

Oliver gave him a blank stare and then stood up. 'It's about time for a drink – the sun's well over the yard arm.' He placed the sponge ceremoniously on the mantelpiece. 'May, I know you won't have anything. Rupert – the malt, I suppose?'

'I think I'd prefer sherry.'

'Manzanilla or Amontillado? Or there's some perfectly filthy Oloroso some damn fool brought me the other day – if you'd prefer that.'

May said, 'The damn fool happened to be my great-nephew Stephen.'

'So it was, my dear, so it was. The arty chap. What'll it be then, my boy?'

'I'll try the filthy Oloroso, if I may.'

'Grandad, can I give you a hand?' Miranda said, rising.

'Thank you, my dear. I shan't say no. And what's your tipple?'

Miranda approached the oak chest. 'Whisky, if there's any going.'

'Whisky?' He paused in the act of pouring Rupert's sherry. 'Ummm. I keep forgetting you're all of twenty-three.'

'Twenty-five next month.' She smiled. 'Do whisky drinking young women shock you?'

'Not at all – not at all. Your grandmother has drunk whisky as long as I've known her – and that's well over fifty years. Fifty years,' he said, putting a substantial shot of whisky in each rummer, 'of unblemished harmony.'

May poked the poufe with her stick. 'Come and sit here by me, Miranda.'

'Thank you,' said Rupert, taking his sherry from Oliver.

'Well, try it, my boy, try it,' he watched Rupert closely.

Rupert sipped – sweet as black treacle with a faint hint of resin.

'Well – how is it?'

'Delectable.' Rupert smiled. 'Quite delectable.'

'Ha!'

'You have the same birthday as my mother,' May said to Miranda now perched uneasily on the poufe. 'Did you know that?'

'I think you told me – didn't you all used to go out and pick flowers in the woods on the day?'

'Violets. I can remember the smell now. That's about as much as I can do with smell nowadays – remember. It's the same with taste too. I expect it's got something to do with all these pills I take, don't you?'

'Well . . . perhaps,' Miranda said dubiously. 'It must have been lovely.'

'It *was* lovely,' May said. 'Although it would have been lovelier without my mother. I never got on with my mother, you see – rather like you with yours – I'm afraid she always thought I was cocky. She used to wash out my mouth with soapy water. Evil speaking she used to call it. I never really understood what she meant.'

'May's mother,' said Oliver, lowering his half-empty glass, 'was a thoroughly spiteful old woman.'

'I'm sorry to say that's true. Though mainly to me. We were too much alike, you see. Did you know she died in this house on *my* birthday? She had a stroke in this very chair.'

'She had her stroke in the garden,' Oliver said.

'No, Oliver – where I'm sitting.'

'In a *deck* chair in the garden.'

'In *this* chair – well not actually this very one. My old armchair. It had a purple slip cover, I remember.'

Oliver drained his glass. 'I'm going to have another drink,' he announced, struggling from his chair and waving away Rupert's offer of help. 'Yes, I know what Bowson says,' he said as May pursed her lips, 'but I'm not in the least excited.' He surveyed them truculently. 'There comes the night when the best gets tight and then turns out the guard!' He marched off to the chest, humming.

'I always thought,' continued May placidly, 'that she did it to spite me – on my birthday, you see. We'd had raspberries and cream, we always had raspberries and cream on my birthday. You remember, don't you, Rupert?'

'What? Oh yes. Not that particular time though – I was in Italy. You couldn't get hold of me, so I missed the funeral.' But Little Granny had left him five hundred pounds, which had given him a year's freedom to write the book and recover from Trudi.

'It's perfectly true about the raspberries and cream,' Oliver said loudly, having returned to stand in front of the fire. 'The old lady had taken on board enough to sink a battleship – on top of asparagus and cold salmon and roast lamb and the better part of a bottle of champagne. That's what killed her if anything did. It would kill me.' He paused dramatically. 'All the same, she died in the garden.'

'Yes, dear,' said May. 'Have you quite finished?'

'Quite finished, thank you. Now I'm going to collar Miranda. Come along, my dear, there's something I want to –'

'*I* am having a word with Miranda at the moment – as you can see,' May said. 'You must wait your turn.'

'My turn?' He frowned. 'Oh very well – very well. When your grandmother has done with you, my dear, I shall be in my studio.'

'I'd better be making myself scarce too,' Rupert said as Oliver left the room, grandly bearing his whisky. 'I'll see if I can't give Vi a hand.'

'What a good idea. And you might ask her to find a vase for these.' May passed him the tulips.

From the door he glanced back at Miranda poised on the poufe, wondering what she was in for. The earnest expression, the attitude of total attention, even the glass held tight in her hand (though of milk then, not whisky) touched him with a sharp pang from the past – just so had she sat as a little girl waiting for a story.

'Do you ever do it with garlic?' He leant against the back door, watching Vi lay the leg of lamb in the roasting pan.

'No, I've never done it with garlic,' Vi said uncertainly. Perhaps she didn't know what garlic was.

'You make little incisions with a sharp knife and then push the points of garlic in. The flavour sort of seeps into the meat.'

'Meat,' she echoed, dusting the lamb with flour. 'I don't think your father would like that.'

'Perhaps not.' He realized his fingers were itching to take over – and only yesterday he'd been congratulating himself on never having to cook again. He sighed. 'Vi, you don't suppose there'd be any beer in this house, do you?'

'I think there's some in the garage – your father got some in for young Mister Stephen when he came to lunch.'

There was. A dozen cans of Guinness and ten of Carlsberg – Stephen must have been abstemious. They were in a cardboard box on the seat of May's wheelchair. The spokes were spotted with rust and a shrivelled cobweb hung from the back. Obviously nothing in the garage had been used for a long time – an old bicycle, wicker baskets, huge pans for jam making, mason jars, a perished hose, a boiler for the white wash, a broken mangle – he even spotted his old toy fort perched on a shelf at the back. And hundreds of boxes – and a tin trunk and two tea chests and a Gladstone bag without a handle and stacks of old newspapers neatly tied in bundles.

He picked up three cans of Guinness and, backing out of the garage, locked away the debris of their active lives.

'Would you care for one?' he asked Vi.

'No, thank you very much. I'm on a diet at the moment. Just a piece of cheese and an apple at lunch is all I'm allowed. I've lost two stone since Christmas.'

'Good heavens! Two stone. Marvellous.' And barely credible, he thought.

'It is marvellous. My husband says he hardly knows me. But we always go to Margate for Easter – to a holiday camp, you know – so I expect I shall put it all on again then.' She was busily peeling the potatoes – but not very efficiently – skating over eyes and leaving unpeeled patches.

Rupert pulled the tab of a Guinness – it popped explosively and spray shot onto his shirt.

Vi giggled. 'That reminds me of my father-in-law,' she said. 'Ever so fond of his pint, he was. When I go off, he used to say, I don't want no ruddy flowers lying about on top of me. If you have to put something on my grave, he said, make it a bottle of Bass. Well, of course, Maureen, that's his wife, and my Henry were very shocked at that – and when he popped off they made sure there were plenty of wreaths and bouquets, like a flower show, I said at the time. Then a few months later me and Gloria – that's my sister-in-law – thought we'd go and pay our respects one afternoon. "Let's take him a bottle of Bass," she said. But all I'd got in the house was an old can of Guinness. "That'll do," she said, "he won't know the difference where he is." They'd just put the headstone over him and we stood admiring it. "Ever loving and faithful husband," it said. We had a good laugh over that – he was always one for the girls. Well, after a bit we put the Guinness on him and started walking away – and we'd only gone a few yards when "pop!" off flew the little handle and Guinness frothing all over the marble! "He must have had a thirst on him," I said. "Well he would, wouldn't he?" Gloria said, "knowing where he is most likely." We had a good chuckle over that too.'

Rupert gave a short laugh, although it seemed to him quite unfunny – why exactly, he didn't know. But he'd always found it strangely hard to get the hang of Vi – she was a balloon that slid away at the touch of a hand and wafted off. She had some of the better qualities of humanity – decency, kindness, tolerance, humour, loyalty – and yet she seemed to him humanoid, rather than human. Or was it he who was less than human?

'How do you think my parents have been lately?'

'Oh they have their little ups and downs, you know. What with one thing and another, it's been a hard winter for them. It took your mother ever such a long time to get over her bronchitis.'

'Bronchitis? When was that? I didn't hear about it.'

'Just after Christmas I think it was. She had it quite bad. The

Doctor was coming in every day *and* a lady physiotherapist for a time. The antibiotics got her over it in the end, but it left her very weakly.'

'I didn't know.'

'Mr Darley, he had it too, but not as bad.'

'I expect he made a fuss, all the same.'

'Oh yes – but it wouldn't be the same if he didn't, would it? He said to me one day, "Vi, I think I'm dying." "Oh no, you're not," I said, "I've brought you some crumpets for your tea and I'm not taking them home again." He perked up then. It was the bronchitis that made him give up smoking.'

'You must have – have put in a lot of extra time.'

'I came up whenever I could. I wouldn't like Mrs Darley to pass away while I wasn't there. I've been here twenty-four years next month, you know.'

'Have you? I didn't realize. That's a long time.'

'I always thought, when she does have to go, I want to be holding her in my arms, you see.'

'I see, yes – of course.' He took a long drink of the stout.

Vi put down the peeler and shook the water from her hands. 'What sort of a vase will you be wanting for your tulips then?'

'There used to be a smallish china one with a silver glaze and a holder inside. I thought I'd cut the stems down and put them in that – they'd look rather nice on the dining room table.'

'Table,' she said.

'Now then, my dear, I shall come straight to the point. What I want from you is a little advice about a medical matter.'

Miranda frowned. 'Well, of course I'll help if I can, Granny – but, you know, I'm only in my –'

'Yes yes, my dear, I do understand that you're not qualified or anything of that kind, but I think your opinion is bound to be more informed than a layman's.'

'A bit perhaps.' She hesitated, then nodded briefly. 'Alright then, what's the problem?'

'Well, it seems they think it would be a good idea if I went into hospital for two or three weeks.'

'Why exactly, Granny?'

'I can't tell you *exactly*, dear – that's rather the problem. Of course Dr Bowson has explained it to me, but I'm afraid I'm not very quick on the uptake these days.'

Miranda smiled dryly. 'Well, you must have some idea?'

'I wrote it down when he told me. Now let me see.' Putting on her glasses, she slowly turned the pages of her exercise book. 'Yes. Regulation of pills is the first thing I put down. That's something to do with side-effects, I think, but. . . .'

'Hold on a minute, Granny – let me have a look.' She slid off the poufe and knelt at May's table. She examined the pill bottles in silence, reading the labels, opening one bottle and sniffing it. 'There are rather a lot of them, aren't there? Two three times a day, one morning and evening, one before meals, two at six-hour intervals. . . . How do you keep track of all this?'

'To tell you the honest truth, I don't – at least not very efficiently. I write them down in my little book, but I don't always remember. On the whole I reckon I'm alright if I take them all some time during the day. Of course, I *do* know about the distalgesic.'

Miranda nodded and stood up. 'Tell me about the side-effects?'

'The worst is my inner-workings – they're in a dreadful mix-up. Then sometimes I get very dizzy and think I'm going to pass out, and once or twice I've had great difficulty with my breathing. But whether those are side-effects or just what happens to old ladies, I really couldn't tell you.'

'No, and I'm afraid I can't either.' She picked up her glass and took a swallow of whisky. 'But I expect that's one of the things they want to try and find out. It takes careful monitoring to make sure you take the right thing at the right time. Then they can start to play ab – to vary the mix. They might take you off one drug altogether and put you on something different. Until things are working better and you're more comfortable. But all that can't be done at home, you see.'

'Yes, I do see. Although I don't know about being more

comfortable.' She sighed. 'The other thing they're talking about is physiotherapy.'

'For your knees?'

'Yes,' she glanced at her book. 'Something about building up the muscles – can that be right?' she asked doubtfully.

'Oh yes. Osteo-arthritis is the wearing away of the cartilage between the bones – the knees in your case, which is what makes them stiff. The pain comes from the rubbing of bone against bone. The point of physiotherapy is to develop the muscles to make a sort of cushion to take the place of the cartilage.'

'Oh dear, it sounds most painful – I can hardly bear anyone to touch my knees.'

'They'll give you an umbrella injection – you shouldn't feel a thing.'

'Well – how simple you make it sound, my dear. Now why couldn't Dr Bowson explain it all so clearly?' She smoothed the shawl on her lap. 'Would it really make a difference to my poor old pins?'

Miranda hesitated for a moment. 'Yes, with any luck.' She smiled and sat down on the couch. 'You might even be able to potter round the garden again if all goes well.'

'I'm afraid that would be a rather depressing experience these days. But if it would make it any easier for me on the stairs. . . .'

'Well, you won't be darting up and down half a dozen times a day – but it should help. If it works of course.'

'I see. And I've just persuaded Oliver to have a stairlift installed – at great cost, I may say. But now I shall have to think again. It looks as though I really ought to go, doesn't it?'

'It *will* help you, I think, Granny. It's worth a try,' she said cheerfully. 'After all, never say die.'

'Well, we don't say it, my dear, but we think it all the time. I don't fancy I shall last another winter – at least not a winter like this last one.'

'You're not going to die yet, Granny.'

'That's as may be. But the implications of what you say are quite clear. Hospital might keep me alive a little longer, so to hospital I must go. You've explained it all very well – and I'm going to ask you to help me explain it to Oliver when the opportunity arises.'

'Yes of course I will. But, Granny – going to hospital isn't exactly a matter of – well, of –'

'Of life or death? But that's where you're mistaken, Miranda – it's just what it is.' May took off her glasses and pinched the bridge of her nose between thumb and forefinger. 'Oliver's a good deal younger than me, as you may know, but it's always been the understood thing that he would go first – what with his heart and his kidneys. I haven't been as much use to him as I might have been in this life, so the least I can do is see him out gracefully. He couldn't abide hanging about in this house all by himself, you know.' She stared into the fire made pale by sunlight.

Miranda watched her in silence for a while, then she said quietly. 'What do you *want* to do, Granny?'

'If it were simply a question of my wishes – I should say goodnight to you all and go to bed and never wake up.' She raised her head and her blue-eyed gaze was filled with fierceness. 'But when I die, I want to *die*!'

And then after a pause, she smiled faintly. 'I'll tell you a little story. When my mother had her stroke in the garden, we carried her upstairs and rang Dr Goodman – so appropriately named, I always thought. He said she might hang on for days, even months, but would never be much more than a vegetable. I said I didn't care for that a great deal and I'm sure she wouldn't either. He just nodded, and I went out of the room – and four hours later she passed peacefully away.'

'I think that's done much more often than a lot of people realize.'

'You're not against it?'

'Of course not.'

'Well, you think that and I think that – but I'm afraid your father might not.'

'Why not?'

'Because of his religion.'

'His religion?' Miranda gave a half laugh.

'His Catholicism.'

'Daddy – a *Catholic*?' She looked at May incredulously. 'Oh come on, Granny – you must be joking.'

'Oh no, he was very devout. He was converted when he was in the army, or it might have been just after he came out. Later on he became rather disillusioned – perhaps when his first marriage began to go wrong. And I've heard him say he gave it up long ago. But I don't think one can just "give up" religion – not like drink or smoking. I mean, there's bound to be a lingering effect at the very least, don't you think?'

'I just can't. . . .' Frowning, she stared down at the glass in her hand, then raised it suddenly and drank. 'I know he's a bit naive at times, but. . . .'

'You think it naive to be religious?'

'That's – one way of putting it.'

'How very interesting. All my family were religious. And my father was a clergyman. Looking back on it, I think perhaps he *was* rather naive. Or at least, innocent of the ways of the world. Perhaps these things skip a generation. I've never been able to get on with religion myself, although I had to put up with a great deal of it in my young life. But all that sin and misery and meekness – rather unhealthy, I think it was, and exceedingly undignified. I suppose if I'd ever *felt* sinful, it would be different – but I never have. I always feel God should be spelt G-O-O-D. My dear, I'm afraid I've upset you?'

'No – no, that's alright.' She made a movement as if to brush the sunlight from her face. 'It's just that I can't imagine Daddy. . . .' She gave a small half laugh, '. . . oh, going to confession and – and sprinkling himself with holy water and – and whatever they do.'

'I couldn't say exactly what they do – *my* family was quite low church. Although I do know they're against abortion and birth control – so very silly of them. And thoughtless. Years ago I used to run our local Family Planning Association, and you should have seen the relief of some of those poor women when they realized there was a way out of continual child-bearing. I don't think unnecessary suffering can ever be good for one, do you?'

'I couldn't agree more!' Miranda said vehemently.

May nodded. 'Good. And that brings me round to something I wished to say to you.' She paused. 'What I should like to be sure of is that if the same thing happens to me as happened to my mother – there will be somebody there to say the word as I did for Mum. Do you understand?'

'Yes, I understand.'

'Pulling out the plug, I think they call it.'

Miranda looked slowly round the room, then turned to meet May's unwavering regard. 'Alright, Granny. As soon as I hear anything, I'll come as quick as I can and – and do my best. That's all I can promise, isn't it?'

'I ask for no more, my dear. Well now,' she said, replacing the exercise book and opening her sewing box, 'I expect you would like another drink before you go off and see your grandfather.'

'Yes, I think I would.' She took her glass over to the chest and poured a stiff measure.

'Granny,' she said, coming back to stand in front of the fire, 'if your mother had a stroke in the garden, why did you say it happened in here?'

'Well, my dear,' said May, rattling a box of pins, 'one of the tiresome things about my husband is that he always thinks he's right. So I give him a little poke every now and again – to stop him being so smug.'

Miranda laughed – a clean bright sunny laugh – and took a deep breath. And May began to empty the pins into her new fish plate.

The silver and glasses glittered on the old damask tablecloth he'd dug up from the bottom of the sideboard, and in the centre the tulips shone like Chinese red lacquer in the sun. He drank his Guinness and surveyed the table with pleasure – nothing, as far as he could see, was missing.

Miranda poked her head in the door. 'Hello, Poopa, what are

you up to? Having a quiet tipple? *And* smoking, I see.'

'I was just admiring your tulips. They look ravishing, don't they?'

'Very nice.' She gave a brief nod and turned to go.

'Hey, hang on. I wanted to have a word or two.'

'Sorry. I've got an appointment with Grandad.'

'Well, just a moment. How did it go with May? Did she tell you about the hospital?'

'Yes – among other things. Now I'm going to see what Grandad's got up his sleeve for me.'

'But Milly –'

'Must run – he's probably chewing the carpet by now.'

'Oh blast – alright. Maybe you can give *me* an appointment one of these days.'

'Okay. I'll try to fit you in after lunch.'

Rupert grimaced. He finished his beer and put out his cigarette and went out into the hall. He looked in at the kitchen, which was filled with the odour of meat and a gentle sound of simmering.

There were vague noises from upstairs – Vi making the beds and tidying up. Rupert fished the keys from the brass box and unlocked the front door and stood on the doorstep. There was plenty of time to saunter down to the pub for a pint or two – he could do with the beer, but he was not in the mood for loud voices and cosy laughter and piped music.

By craning forward he could just glimpse the peak of the Hamiltons' roof. What, he wondered, were the Hamiltons having for lunch? Jugged hare was not in season. Perhaps something simple for a Saturday – smoked salmon or a game pie and a bottle of Margaux. At least Mrs Hamilton could cook (unless the jugged hare had been ordered in), unlike Trudi, whose culinary ignorance had about matched her voracity – and not only for food. For the first year they'd lived largely on boiled potatoes, baked beans and powdered eggs, with an occasional curry at the Taj Mahal. Her natural promiscuousness had been encouraged by the large repasts that were the price of her favours. Perhaps things would have been different had be been able to solace her with hampers from Harrods . . . or simply longer drawn-out.

Despite the warmth of the sun, he shivered – a goose tripping across his grave. Maybe a stiff malt would do the trick.

Miranda stared fixedly at the drawing on the wall – it had the look of one of those flat-sided conical glass paperweights despairing children give their fathers at Christmas, only enormously enlarged.

'What,' she said, 'are those funny little green things down there in the corner that look like trees?'

'They are trees – *large* trees.'

'But, Grandad, it must be colossal!'

'It is certainly substantial, my dear.' He smiled and rubbed his hands together. 'Very substantial. It is exactly one thousand metres in height – and at base it will measure very slightly less than two square kilometres.'

'Heavens – and I thought you were going to build it in the garden.'

'The *garden* – in the *garden*!' His voice rose with outrage. 'Good God – the smallest level of all will be *four* times the size of the *garden*.'

'I didn't know.' She looked at him wonderingly. 'It's – well, it's just inconceivable.'

'*I* have conceived it,' he said with mollified grandeur. 'It is going to be my memorial.'

'You mean a kind of, like, mausoleum?'

'No no no no! I do *not* intend to be interred in it.'

'But I thought that was what a pyramid was for – didn't the Egyptians –'

'I am not bound by what the Egyptians did or did not do. The pyramid is one of the oldest and grandest forms of architecture known to mankind. The Babylonians were building pyramids long before the Egyptians came on the scene – the Tower of Babel was one. The Hindus used the same principle – and quite independently in America, the Mayas and the Toltecs and later the Aztecs built pyramidal structures of vast extent.' He blew out his cheeks and waved a hand skyward. 'Vast extent. . . .'

'Grandad, it's brilliant – you must be feeling terrific!'

Oliver smiled faintly. 'I am pleased, yes – I'm exceedingly pleased. It has taken me, you know, almost seven years to the day.'

'Seven years!'

'Yes, I've done everything myself, you see,' he said, rubbing his fingers as though to ease the ache of that long labour, 'everything. I wasn't going to have them say Darley couldn't do his own work. There's no doubt it's a major achievement. Of course, there are one or two things to be done before I die – one or two things. . . .' His voice dwindled. He seemed suddenly to have run out of steam.

'Grandad, are your hands cold?'

'My hands are always cold.'

'Here.' Miranda took his hands and began gently to massage them.

'If only I were fifty years younger,' he said, looking out of the window where the sun shone on the tufted lawn and silvered the soft grey bark of the apple trees and a scavenging seagull scattered the sparrows from the bird table. 'Darley's folly,' he murmured.

'Folly?' she said, smiling.

'That's what they'll call it – my pyramid.' He laughed.

'But what a super folly!'

He nodded, warming slowly. 'I pride myself on never doing the expected. I remember when I won the competition to rebuild Hurstfield Parish Church, they all said, Darley's an atheist, Darley never had an ecclesiastical thought in his head, what does Darley know? And I said, I may know nothing about faith, but I know what a church is – a church is a machine for praying in! That made 'em sit up and take notice.'

'And so will the Pyramid.'

'Ah – the Pyramid. Perhaps. But it won't be built in my lifetime – nor indeed in your father's. But possibly by the time you're my age – or even Rupert's age – people may have come round to seeing a little sense. So that's why I am going to entrust you with the whole caboodle.'

'*Me*?' She stilled her hands on his.

'Yes, my dear – you. I am bequeathing the entire project to you – to your charge, that is. Plans, drafts, drawings, all my notes and sketches, the daily diary of my progress – the lot. There is, I may say, a considerable mass of material – most in fact of what is in this studio. And the model of course – old Butterfield is making the model, on a scale of one to five hundred, and he tells me it is going well and . . . why, my dear, what's the matter?'

'Grandad,' she said, her voice quavering on a note of unconcealed dismay. 'Grandad, I'm terribly flattered – of course I am – but –'

'Flattery doesn't enter into it. You –'

'But, I'm not an architect – honestly, I'm a complete ignoramus.'

'That doesn't matter – you can learn.'

'Wouldn't it be better,' she persisted, 'to have somebody who knew about your work – Daddy, for instance?'

'Your father, Miranda, is an intelligent man. He is a highly talented humorist – or was – but –'

'Oh, he's still reeling off light verse, you know, and doing his bits and pieces for *Punch* and –'

'*Punch*?' Oliver freed his hands. 'My dear, I have chosen you because what matters is that you're young and practical and you have vision. Oh I know yours is a socialist vision – not my kind at all – but anyone of the slightest intelligence is a socialist when they're young. I was myself – rabid, absolutely rabid.'

'You?' Miranda smiled. 'Oh Grandad!'

'But I assure you, it's true.' He laughed lightly. 'I saw visions and dreamed dreams. I was never seriously seduced by the Bolsheviks, but I voted Labour in every election till 1935 – when I got fed up with their pacifism. May and I had spent a year in Germany by then, and I knew what the Nazis were all about. I knew we'd have to fight again if we were to preserve any vestige of civilization.'

He paused, looking at Miranda intently. 'I may be an old fogey now, fiddling about until I die, but I still believe in progress and the ennoblement of mankind – unfashionable ideas these days, I know, but their time will come again. Make no mistake about *that*.'

Miranda did not answer at once. She stood looking at the glass case of medals on the wall above the mantelpiece – not medals of war, but mementos of peaceful achievement.

'I see,' she murmured. She turned back to him. 'Alright, Grandad, then you'd better tell me all about the Pyramid.'

Oliver pulled down his rumpled sweater and cleared his throat. 'As you will observe, it is an octagonal pyramid, and the basic principle of construction is of course the space-frame – a modified utilization of Makowski's space-grid – in which the individual elements are allowed to express the form of the whole. The members will be mainly of anodized aluminium, while the surface area will consist of more than five square kilometres of glass, plastic and solar panelling.'

He picked up a steel rule and stepped closer to the plan. 'It will have,' he said, 'over three hundred separate levels. . . .'

'Shall I dish up now, Madam, or should I wait?'

May paused in her sewing – she was turning an old linen sheet. 'Are they still closeted in there, Vi?'

'I think they are, Madam. Shall I go and have a look?'

'No, I think not – we can leave them to get on with it a little longer. But you can ring the gong now. If they still aren't out, you can dish up and ring the gong again in five minutes.'

'Five minutes. Yes, Madam.'

'Oh and Vi – don't trouble to wait after that, you get on home.'

'Oh I don't mind stopping. I can do the washing up.'

'Milly and I'll see to that,' Rupert said from the corner where he was pouring whisky into his glass.

'Are you sure?' Vi looked enquiringly at May.

'Yes, that's much the best plan. And we'll settle up on Monday morning, if you don't mind.'

Rupert sat down in Oliver's chair. When Vi had left, he said, 'wouldn't it be possible for Vi to stay for the afternoons as well – I mean, it's only for two weeks?'

'Well it might be, yes. And of course Hazel Maybury would be only too glad to look in from time to time, and I'm sure Mrs Hamilton on the other side would make his suppers for him – and Peggy will bring the Sunday lunch, as she always does when we're by ourselves. It's just that he's not used to being alone – and what if something happens in the middle of the night?'

'How about getting someone to sleep in? A nurse or. . . .'

In the hall, the brazen note of the gong swelled and diminished.

'. . . or a baby-sitter?'

'My dear, have you any notion of what that would cost? Besides, you know how he feels about strangers in the house.' She licked thumb and forefinger, raised the needle to the light and re-threaded it with a steady hand.

'Maybe he'll be able to come up with a solution himself – after all, he is a reasonable man at bottom.'

'Huh!'

Rupert drank in silence, watching her sew.

'Are you going to tackle him after lunch?' he said after a while.

'I was going to. But you can see how excited he is already – and he'll drink too much at lunch and won't be fit for anything for the rest of the day, if I know Oliver. I might be able to broach it this evening, but I'm very much afraid we'll have to leave it till tomorrow – before he's had the chance to get too stimulated.'

'Before he's had a drink, in other words?'

'Yes, dear. Well, I think that's quite enough on that subject for the moment. Now tell me about your future plans.'

'My future plans?' Rupert drank some malt and lit a cigarette, making a slow business of it. He cleared his throat. 'Well,' he said.

'. . . regulating its own atmosphere and creating its own climate.'

His shoulders straight, his chin raised so the heavy jowls were smoothed away, Oliver spoke with swift, brisk clarity, without a trace of the cracked tone of age.

'It will have gardens and lakes, trees and plants and flowers and fruit and bees and beetles and butterflies and birds and animals, both domestic and wild.'

'And human beings?'

'And human beings. It will be capable of supporting fifty thousand people in total comfort and productive ease – naked if so desired. And also, living quarters for them – and workshops and libraries and theatres. It will even have a distillery. It will contain everything for the arts and manufactures of mankind, for creation and recreation. Heat and cold, night and day, music and silence!'

'It sounds like a paradise – like the garden of Eden.'

'Better – no serpent!'

They laughed, and he threw down the ruler with a clatter. At the same moment the gong resounded from the hall.

'Dear me,' he said, 'I'm afraid they are getting impatient. Let us repair to the refectory and stoke up.'

'Okay,' Miranda said. Smiling she took his proffered arm and leaned up and kissed his cheek.

'Ah,' he said. 'And perhaps before we sit down, you'd get me a whisky from the sitting room – *not* the malt.'

'Here? In this house?' said Miranda disbelievingly.

'Certainly. We always had music in this house.' Oliver tucked his napkin under his chin and picked up his knife and fork. 'Still would have – only I've never learnt how to manipulate that damned radiogram or whatever it's called.'

'Oh – when did you get it? I thought it had been there forever.'

'May, when did we get that radiogram thing in the sitting room?'

May was cutting her meat into small morsels. 'Not long after the war, I think. I'd say we've had it well over thirty years.'

'Thirty years – and you haven't. . . .' Miranda's laughter rang out.

Oliver smiled. 'Rupert knows how to make it work, don't you, Rupert?'

'It hardly takes a mechanical genius.'

'I know how to make it work, too,' May said.

'I expect you do, my dear – but then you don't like music.'

'I don't know why you say that. I'm very fond of certain hymns.'

'So am I – but not in the sitting room.' He reached out for his whisky glass. 'When we had the old gramophone which could be wound up, I used to play a lot of music – Beethoven, Grieg, Mozart, Haydn. When he was a very small boy, Rupert used to dance to it.'

'Daddy – dancing? Did you really, Poopa?'

'I do vaguely remember twirling round and round and getting very dizzy.'

'There was a particular record that used to set you off – one of Greig's Norwegian Dances, I think it was. We thought you might turn out to be musical – set you to learning the flute.'

'The recorder.'

'Yes, well. But of course that idea was killed stone dead when we sent you to that frightful school – May, what was the name of that frightful school we sent Rupert to?'

'The Rudolph Steiner school. I wonder if I might –'

'That's it – Steiner.' Oliver drank some whisky. 'What a disaster that was. You weren't there for long. In fact music was the principle reason we took you away. We went to hear the school concert –'

May said, 'I just want to ask –'

'Yes yes, my dear – pray allow me to finish what I am saying. It must have been the end of term or half term or something – and the music master, who was quite a well-known musician at the time although I don't recall his name –'

'Edmund Rubbra,' Rupert said.

'Yes, that's it.' Oliver picked up the wine bottle and filled his wine glass. 'Well, all the children came onto the stage with their fiddles and flutes and oboes and what-not and proceeded to play whatever they liked. And this chap Rubber just stood there and allowed them to do it – they were supposed to be expressing themselves or something. I've never heard such a cacophony in my entire life.' He raised his glass. 'So that was the end of that!'

'Have you quite finished now?'

'What, my dear?' He put up a hand to shield his eyes against the glare of the sun. 'Oh yes, I've quite finished, thank you.'

'In that case – Miranda, I wonder if I could trouble you for the red currant jelly?'

'Oh Granny – have you been wanting it all this time?'

'Anyone care for meat?' Rupert asked. 'Oliver, your plate looks empty.'

'Thank you, my boy, I wouldn't say no. May, my dear, I do wish you wouldn't interrupt me when I'm in the middle of saying something.'

'Isn't that rather the pot calling the kettle black?'

'What pot? What are you talking about?'

Rupert placed two slices of lamb on Oliver's plate. 'Anything interesting happened in the road lately?' he asked genially.

'No, I don't think so.' May helped herself to a speck of red currant jelly. 'I expect I've told you about the Robinsons, haven't I?'

'The Robinsons – pah!'

'Well, Oliver, you said you liked *her*.'

'I always like American women – at least they're alive.'

'Well, of course I could hardly be expected to know about that. But it is rather a funny story. We went to dinner there – at Tudor Lodge, you know – it must have been a week or two before Christmas, at any rate it was the last time we went out.'

'Or ever likely to,' Oliver muttered with his mouth full.

'There were eight of us and it was all extremely grand, not at all the sort of thing we're accustomed to these days – lace tablecloth and napkins and candles and three glasses each. Very superior, I must say – but then the Americans rather go in for all that, don't they? Although *he* of course was English.'

'A wet smack, if ever I saw one.'

'A most agreeable man, quite a proper person, I thought. Well, we all sat down, with those odd little bowls of salad Americans always put beside your plate – lettuce, you know, with half a tinned peach and what I think they call cottage cheese, really quite off-putting.'

'Dog's vomit.'

'And then Mr Robinson came round with the wine – in a basket, with a napkin round the neck. So I said to him, "You're very professional, aren't you?" Then he leant down and whispered in my ear – "It's more than my life's worth to spill a drop on this tablecloth – it's an heirloom." Well, it can't have been more than a few minutes afterwards that I said something vehement and made an appropriate gesture,' May gave a brisk little flip of her hand, 'and poff! – over went my glass, and a great pool of wine –'

'A first-class claret, I may say,' Oliver remarked, pouring himself some more Burgundy.

'"Oh, I am sorry," I said. "Oh not a bit of it," said Mrs Robinson with the most angelic of smiles, "think nothing of it – it really couldn't matter less." Of course I suggested salt and white wine and all the things one's used to doing, but she would have none of it, simply spread a napkin over the stain. So I just left it at that – though I don't mind telling you I gave old Mr Robinson a wink.'

'Not so old – about your age, Rupert.'

'Really, it was enough to make a cat laugh.'

'*I* was sorry for Robinson,' Oliver said firmly.

'And as it turned out, you were quite right,' said May. 'It wasn't so long after that Mr Robinson made away with himself.'

Rupert stopped eating. 'He *what*?'

Miranda made a hiccoughing noise, but kept her head well down.

'Committed suicide. He shut himself in the garage with the car motor running. Of course they said it was an accident – but then they always do, don't they? But one would have to be exceptionally incompetent to die like that by accident – and on the whole Mr Robinson struck me as rather a practical man.'

Rupert ran his finger round the rim of his glass. 'That's a pretty gruesome tale.'

'Is it? Yes, I suppose it is in a way,' May said reflectively. 'I sometimes wonder if he did it because of the wine.'

Miranda's giggles got the better of her and her shoulders shook uncontrollably.

'All I can say is, thank God I never learnt to drive,' Oliver said. 'Is there any pudding?'

'Stewed pears and custard.'

'Then I shall stick to cheese.'

'I'm sorry,' Miranda said, drying her eyes on her napkin. 'I don't know what . . . I'm not usually giggly.' And then she was shaken by another attack.

'Don't worry, my dear, humour takes us all in different ways. Rupert – you're the expert – haven't you something to amuse us?'

'As a matter of fact I did hear a story at the Club yesterday about. . . .' He hesitated, glancing at May. 'No – on second thoughts, perhaps not.'

'Oh Daddy, don't be such a stick-in-the-mud.'

'Come on, my boy, out with it!'

'Well – alright. Of course, you don't know the washrooms at the Club – they're very large and spacious, but they've been in a squalid state for quite a few years. So finally the Committee decided to spend a bit of money on refurbishing – it must have been quite a lot of money, actually. They retiled the floor, put in new washbasins and taps – though they kept the old marble surrounds of course – new mahogany lavatory seats, new mirrors, repainted everything, even to putting a bit of gilt on top of the Doric columns –'

'Ionic,' said Oliver, flapping his hand against the sun.

'Well, anyway – shortly after it'd all been done, two very elderly members were standing at the urinals, you know – "Morning, Teddy. . . . Morning, Fitz." "I say, old boy, all this is pretty impressive, eh?" – nods at the new decor. "Mmm, yes – yes. Makes the old cock look a bit shabby, what?"'

There was a moment of hush – May looking puzzled, Miranda giving her father a sad little smile.

Oliver screwed up his eyes. 'Joke over – ha ha!'

'Grandad, is the sun bothering you?'

'Yes, my dear, it always does at this time of day at this particular time of the year.'

'I'll pull down the blind.'

'Would you? I should be most grateful.'

'I'm afraid I never understand these jokes about balls and cocks and bottoms,' said May, as Miranda went to the window. 'Is it very funny?'

'Oh, let it pass, my dear, let it pass.' Oliver cut himself a large slice of cheddar.

The blind was old and sent out little gouts of dust as it was lowered, and the light shining through it lent Oliver's features a bloody cast.

'What, porter, ho! Let the portcullis fall!' he cried. 'Thank you, my dear, thank you. Yes, I've always liked that story. I think it was Moncrieff-Todd who first told it – must be all of twenty-five years ago.'

'Oh,' said Rupert, 'I thought it was new.'

'Old as the hills, but none the worse for that. Of course, he's dead now – Moncrieff-Todd. Everyone's dying like flies these days.' He broke a water biscuit. 'I think a glass of port would go down very well – if there's any left. One for the road, as they say – a resonant phrase.' He beamed bloodily about him. 'Not that I intend going anywhere of course.'

'Let's go this way,' said Miranda, starting briskly down the narrow path flanked by dead bracken. The ground was soaking with yesterday's rains, but she had found an old pair of Wellingtons in the bottom of the hall cupboard and strode confidently down the hill.

Rupert hesitated, then followed her with a shrug – his shoes were already sodden.

'So it isn't really all that serious,' he said.

'It's not critical,' she answered over her shoulder, 'if that's what you mean. But anything's *serious* at their age – or could be.'

'It would be marvellous if she could get up and down stairs again properly.'

'Don't expect miracles, Daddy.'

The path widened and he caught up with her. 'No, I don't expect miracles, but at least it will be an improvement.'

'Oh yes – if it works. Any exercise is better than none. Sitting in that chair all day – well, she's only got to catch a cold and it's an open invitation to pneumonia or bronchitis and then. . . .'

'She had bronchitis earlier this year.'

'I know. They both did.'

'Vi said it hit her harder than him.'

'Maybe.'

'What does that mean?'

'It means it's difficult to tell. He bounces about in a way she can't, but his colour's not good and he drinks far too much – God knows what his kidneys are like. It's a toss-up which one of them goes first.'

They had reached the bottom of the declivity and now began to mount the slope on the other side. He gave her a considering look. 'Milly, I sometimes wonder what on earth possessed you to take up medicine.'

'Do you?' She slowed for a moment. 'Look, Daddy – hospital or no hospital, it's not going to make all that difference. It'll only prolong the agony, or postpone it if you want to think of it that way. With any luck, she's just going to drop dead one of these days – upstairs or downstairs or in the loo, I don't see that it matters much where, so long as it's not week after week in some intensive care unit.'

'That's pretty brutal.'

'It's not brutal to look truth square in the face.' She turned her head to him. '*They* do – or at least, Granny does. But she's got guts.'

'Yes,' he said, conscious of the implied rebuke. He was breathing hard from the mild climb – extraordinary what only a couple of days smoking could do to one's wind. 'Yes,' he repeated, 'but I was really talking about your attitude.'

'It wouldn't help your patients if you tried to take on their sufferings – besides which, it would drive you out of your mind.'

'May and Oliver are your grandparents, not your patients.'

'Don't I know it.' They were on the brow of the hill now, and she stopped and faced him. 'Why else do you think I'm here?'

Rupert looked down at the small valley where Bog Lodge nestled cosily. The time had come to tell her his news. There was a disconcerting stoniness in her manner already – perhaps she had already guessed what he was going to say. He took a deep breath – and coughed.

'What did Oliver want?' he asked, putting off the moment.

'He wanted to tell me about his pyramid.'

'Oh. That's all?'

'That's all.'

'I see. Milly, there's something I want to. . . .'

A large auburn dog came bounding across the road, narrowly missing a car.

'Elsa – Elsa!' came an anguished cry from the other side of the road, as Rupert stepped back from the dog's muddy-footed assault.

'Good God,' he said, 'it's Mrs Hamilton.'

'Who's she?' said Miranda, firmly pushing the dog away.

'Mrs Hamilton – from next door, she's –'

'Oh dear, I am so sorry!' Mrs Hamilton had scurried over the road and now seized the dog by its collar. 'Mr Darley, you must forgive me, but –'

'Rupert – please. Mr Darley's my father.' Rupert smiled. 'And this is my daughter, Miranda. Mrs Hamilton.'

'How do you do, Miranda?' She was wearing a beautifully cut suit of crimson and dark blue tweed.

'How do you do, Mrs Hamilton?' said Miranda with a faint smile.

'Oh, Emma – you must call me Emma.'

Rupert laughed. 'I'm sorry,' he said, as she flushed suddenly. 'It's just that – well, Emma Hamilton, you know.'

'Oh yes – I *do* know. Everyone thinks it is amusing – and I am a diplomat's wife too. But I am always sorry for Lady Hamilton.'

'And quite right too – they treated her shockingly badly.'

'Yes.' She smiled shyly, as if in some way she had been paid a compliment. 'I hope your mother liked the flowers.'

'Oh yes – she loved them. She said to thank you very much. She's tremendously fond of flowers, you know.'

They stood in silence, as the dog wrenched and pulled to get free, but Mrs Hamilton had a surprisingly strong hand.

Rupert caught Miranda's eye and looked away; he cleared his throat.

'Gorgeous day, isn't –'

'Well, I must be –'

'Sorry.'

'No no – please,' Mrs Hamilton said earnestly, 'it *is* a very beautiful day. So clear.'

They turned and looked at the view across London. The rain had cleansed the air, and sunshine and distance lent a certain amount of enchantment to the high-risers that littered the City.

Rupert said, 'I remember when the tallest thing you could see was St Paul's – and the Tower of London, of course.'

'Why of course?' said Miranda.

'Oh, because it was here – or rather on the little hillock behind us on the other side of Sidmouth Wood – that Henry VIII stood on the morning of Anne Boleyn's execution. He rode over from Hampton Court and, as soon as she got the chop, they fired a cannon from the Tower so he could see the puff of smoke and know the job was done.'

'How very interesting,' Mrs Hamilton said.

'I suppose he couldn't enjoy his breakfast until he knew he'd murdered his wife,' Miranda said dryly.

Mrs Hamilton's eyes widened with surprise. 'But she had been very naughty, hadn't she?'

'Not as naughty as him.' Rupert laughed.

'Or as Lady Hamilton,' said Miranda.

Mrs Hamilton looked from one to the other and slowly smiled. Then the dog tore loose and plunged down the slope wild with barks.

'Oh dear. Elsa – Elsa! I am afraid I must go.' And Mrs Hamilton darted after her dog.

She did not run gracefully, but then who can run gracefully downhill? She had fine strong hands and pretty eyes and, Rupert guessed, a sense of mischief beneath the awkwardness of a foreign language. All signs that could be, probably were, misleading; after all, he was an expert at misjudgement. He sighed.

'Do you fancy her, Daddy?'

He turned to her in time to catch a sardonic glance. He shook his head, not in denial, but clearing his mind.

'I've left your mother, Milly,' he said, and then, as she stared at him without a word, 'That's why I came here – to tell the old folk.'

'And me?' she said quietly.

'I wrote to you at your flat. I didn't know you'd be here. I'm sorry.'

'Why should you be sorry?'

'I'm afraid it's a bit of a shock, but –'

'It's not a shock. Not to me. I thought you'd never do it – still, better late than never. But why now, after all these miserable years?'

'Miserable?' He looked speculatively across the valley. Up the slope on the other side Mrs Hamilton was still pursuing her dog. But it had been sharper than misery – cold steel in the night, and clawing as though, what was that line of Ransom's? – as though there were individual tigers in their blood trying to get undone. So why any particular time, any particular words . . . ?

'It was something Mum said a few weeks ago – not long after Christmas, as a matter of fact. I had old Petrie in for a glass of sherry – you remember Petrie?'

'Don't I just – he always used to feel me up when I was little.'

'*Petrie* did? Not when I was there!'

'But you weren't there a lot of the time, were you? Off on your stupid guided tours.'

'But look here, are you sure? Petrie's a –'

'Respectable married man with three kids and a dog and a Ford Cortina – oh come *on*, Daddy! One day I slapped his fat face and knocked his glasses off – *then* he stopped.'

'Good Lord.' He laughed briefly. 'Then perhaps your mother had something after all.'

'Why? What happened?'

'Oh – well, there we were drinking our sherry and suddenly she comes into the room, takes one look at us and says, "You are oppressors of women!" Just like that. And then she goes out and slams the door. But she said it, you know, with such utter conviction that –'

'Of course she did – because she was *right*.'

'Now wait a minute. I. . . .' He took a deep breath to cool a quick surge of anger. 'Why do you say that?'

'You practically snatched her from the cradle, put her in the family way, left her alone while you went jaunting off abroad, then expected her to dance attendance on you when you did settle down – mother and household slave and a dutiful schoolmaster's wife! Christ, Daddy, if it hadn't been for you, she'd be a professor now instead of just a lecturer at the local poly. You *have* been oppressing her – you *are* an oppressor!'

'It was obvious she felt that very deeply, but –'

'But you still haven't grasped that marriage is *the* basic form of oppression for women.'

'It sometimes isn't so hot for men either.'

Miranda made a quick dismissive gesture. 'I don't know why you two got married in the first place – you've so obviously got nothing in common. I suppose it was on the rebound.'

Rupert laughed. 'My dear Milly, if you'd ever known Trudi, you might have wondered it didn't put me off marriage for good and all.' He moved to take her arm, but she stepped back sharply.

'God, Daddy, can't you take anything seriously?'

'What do you mean?' He frowned, puzzled. 'What's got into you?'

'Even your book about the war was frivolous.'

'You've read it?' He smiled with surprised pleasure. 'Well, you know, frivolity can be the height of seriousness.'

'Who said that? Oscar Wilde?'

'I don't think so – he'd have said it better.'

'And do you wonder why you drove Mum half out of her skull?'

He turned away. He felt suddenly tired. Mrs Hamilton had vanished, but there were other people, other dogs on the hillside now, and a brace of children in brightly coloured Wellington boots.

'Then I suppose it was sex.'

'What? What was?' He blinked at her. 'What are you talking about?'

'Why you married Mum.'

'Oh. That isn't such a bad reason.' He pulled himself together. He hadn't expected it would be quite as bad as this. 'In point of fact we got married because you were on the way.'

'And I suppose abortion would have been against your sacred Catholic principles.'

'Catholic principles?' He shook his head slowly. 'I wasn't much of a Catholic by that time. Anyway, we had you because we wanted you.'

'Daddy, how *could* you have been a Catholic – *you* of all people?'

'It wasn't easy – and I was never very good at it. . . .' He rubbed his face with one hand. 'May must have been talking to you about it – or was it Oliver?'

'Granny mentioned it.'

'Yes of course – Oliver isn't a gossip.'

'It wasn't gossip.'

'Oh?'

'It just cropped up in the course of conversation.'

Like mother, like daughter, he had thought a few moments ago, but now, observing the steady blue gaze of her eyes and the sharp cut of the nose, it was May she resembled the more. And there was no one like May for telling a lie without blenching.

He said, 'Let's go into Richmond and buy some crumpets for tea.'

'Oh there you are at last.' May, on the edge of her chair, sank back, a look of exhaustion on her face. 'Miranda, I wonder if you would just pop upstairs and see what the old boy wants – he's been thumping away for the last ten minutes.'

'I'll go,' Rupert said quickly.

'I think it would be better if Miranda went.'

'Okay, Granny. Here, Daddy, catch!' She tossed the brown paper bag to Rupert and left the room.

'What's that you've got there?' May said.

'Crumpets.'

May gave a slight shudder. 'Lift my legs onto the footstool, would you, my dear? Gently,' she said, watching with apprehension.

Despite his care, she gasped as he raised her feet and slipped the footstool under her calves.

'I'm sorry,' he said.

'It's not your fault – ouch!' She winced.

'Hadn't you better take a couple of painkillers?'

'No, I took two after lunch. I shall have to wait a little longer now.'

'I'll make us some tea – perhaps that would help.'

May gave a small smile and shook her head. She put on her glasses and looked at Rupert. 'Why, my dear, you're absolutely sopping.'

From the knees down he was soaked and there were damp patches on the carpet where he had trodden.

'You should have borrowed Oliver's old boots.'

'Or kept the bottoms of my trousers rolled.'

'I don't think that would have been very sensible. You'd better go and change.'

'Yes.' He hesitated. 'Will you be alright? Can I get you anything?'

'Quite alright, thank you, my dear. But perhaps a hot water bottle if it wouldn't be too much trouble.'

She waited until the door shut behind him, then took off her glasses and closed her eyes.

'Oh dear, oh dear, oh dear,' she murmured to the empty room.

'What is it, Grandad?' she asked urgently.

He sat on the edge of the bed, supporting himself with one hand on the bedside table and the other grasping the scabbarded sword he used to bang the floor with.

'Pills,' he gasped.

'Where are they?' And then she saw them scattered on the carpet, spilled from the shell-shaped silver box he carried them in. She gathered them quickly.

'Open your mouth – there.' She put one under his tongue.

He grunted and relaxed his hand so the sword fell to the floor, slithering from the scabbard. Miranda wrapped the eiderdown round his shoulders and sat beside him on the bed and took his hand in hers.

He turned his head towards her slowly. 'Be alright in a minute or two,' he whispered. His eyes were like blue jewels, bright with the innocence of old age.

'Of course you will.' She stroked his hand. 'It's just one of your angina attacks, isn't it?'

He nodded. 'Warm hands. . . .' He closed his eyes.

Miranda looked out of the window. From where she sat only the tops of the yet unbudded trees in the Park were visible – and the sky clouded over to a uniform grey. Already, coming back from their walk, the afternoon had grown chilly, and the bedroom now struck cold and gloomy. With her foot she manoeuvred the sword back into its scabbard and pushed it under the bed where it clanged gently against a chamber pot. Stale urine was part of the bedroom smell, mingling with the scent of linen and lavender and tweed and shoe polish and bay rum and dust – dust from the books in shelves and on every spare surface. Beside the restored pillbox on the bedside table, the Rhodes sponge rested on top of a volume of the *Strand Magazine* for 1897. The room had an ancient and unsolaced air, without even the Victorian comfort of a double bed. And the house was utterly still, even from outside there was no sound –

presumably the entire suburb had retired to tea and crumpets and Saturday TV sport.

'Better?' she said as Oliver opened his eyes.

'Much better, thank you. Stupid of me to knock them on the floor. I'm most frightfully clumsy these days – must be an early form of senility, I suppose.'

'Early?' Miranda smiled.

'Not so early.' He laughed. 'I sometimes think it would simplify matters if I left them off altogether – the pills, I mean.' He freed his hand and ran it over the top of his head. 'Christ, I must look a sight.'

'A bit dishevelled.'

'It's this damn hair – all over the place.'

'Would you like me to trim it for you?'

'You? Do you know how?'

'Oh yes, I cut all my friends' hair.'

'*Women*'s hair.'

'Men's too.'

'Well in that case. . . .' He hesitated, then took the plunge. 'Then I don't see why not. After all, it can't do much harm.'

Miranda laughed.

'I'm afraid that sounded a bit ungracious. It's just that I shouldn't like to upset Mr Mason – he's been doing my hair for forty years, you know, first at Trumper's and then. . . . Come to think of it, to hell with Mason – he's only a barber, dammit. Now?'

'Why not – if you're up to it?'

'Oh I'm up to it alright. But perhaps you'd better light the gas fire first.'

'Let's do it in the living room – it's already nice and warm down there.'

'I'm not sure May would care for that. Mason generally does it in here.'

Hunched in the ancient eiderdown, his hair awry, his cheeks and eye pouches pendulous with age, he looked like the last surviving high priest of some long-forgotten religion.

'I think it would do Granny good to know that you're alright.'

'There is that, I suppose. Well, anything you say.' He regarded her silently for a moment. 'You're a kind-hearted sort of person, aren't you? Like your father.'

'Oh, Daddy's kind, alright.' She got up and went over to the window. The cloud cover had thickened and two or three cars that passed already had their lights on against the coming night. The evening had settled into a steady drizzle.

'Grandad,' she said, turning, 'Grandad, what was Daddy's first wife like?'

'Trudi? Ravishing – absolutely ravishing.' He smiled reminiscently. 'German, you know – he picked her up when he was in the army – but the very opposite of your strapping blond goddess. Dark and comely, with eyes like a young doe's. Not much between the ears, but what ears! She had a somewhat elfin look and an absolutely marvellous figure. God knows how she managed it – she ate like a horse. Gone to seed by now, I expect – beer and bratwurst and sauerkraut – like a proper *hausfrau.* But she'd left Rupert before there was any sign of that of course.'

'Why did she leave him?'

'Ummm? Well, one didn't enquire too closely, you know. Fresh woods and pastures new, I imagine. Life here wasn't quite what she expected – I think she'd thought Rupert was some kind of English milord. There wasn't a great deal to eat, and the Germans were none too popular directly after the war. It was torture to listen to her mangling the language, but she had a way with her – a very definite way.' He chuckled. 'So she will have done all right.'

'And Daddy – how did he take it?'

Oliver blew out his cheeks. 'Hit him rather hard, I'm afraid. Messed up his degree – he ought to have got a first, you know. He went off to Italy. We were quite worried about him. I may say it crossed my mind at that time he might decide to become a monk or a Jesuit. As it turned out, he wrote a rather funny book instead – which I suppose says something for the public school system.'

'Why do you think he married her in the first place?'

'Lust, I should think.' He looked at her meditatively. 'In some ways she was not unlike your mother – physically, I mean. Of course, it's a fundamental mistake to marry merely for sexual gratification. But if it's not impertinent, why do you ask?'

'I don't know.' Miranda moved away from the window. 'Yes, I do. I expect Daddy's told you he's left Mum, and I –'

'Left Sylvia? What do you mean, "left her"?'

'Gone – split up. Left.'

'Has he indeed? Well well. No, he didn't tell me.'

'Oh – then perhaps I shouldn't have told you either.'

'Don't worry about that. It's hardly going to break my heart. With all due deference to your feelings, although I've always greatly admired and respected your mother, I never thought she would be the easiest person in the world to live with.'

Miranda laughed and picked up the sponge and kneaded it gently.

'Besides,' he went on, 'when you're as old as I am, other people's passionate concerns seem rather remote. I don't say one's not touched, but one isn't engaged.'

'But you are engaged.' She looked down at him seriously. 'Before lunch in the studio you said you'd still got lots of things to do.'

'Hardly *lots*, my dear – but, ah, you think I'm being inconsistent?'

'Aren't you?'

'I admit it. But it's one of the great privileges of old age to be totally inconsistent.'

She shook her head obstinately. 'But you did mean what you said?'

'I mean everything I say.' He reached out and took the sponge from her and held it to himself. 'Let me put it this way. When you arrive at my age, there is not a great deal worth living for. One is, it is true, a kind of container of ancient memories – which may be of passing interest to one or two people; there is an American professor, for instance, who is constantly ringing up and wanting to come down and interview me – fortunately your grandmother is a splendid liar and according to her I am perpetually at death's door. But memories are for other people, I take no pleasure in them myself. What else is there? I drink, but I take precious little pleasure in alcohol. I have utterly lost my taste for tobacco. It's true that I enjoy food – I confess it, I am even greedy. Your grandmother, poor dear, has lost even that appetite – but she is of stouter material than I. I am fortified by neither faith nor optimism. I have always believed that human affairs would go from bad to worse, and by and large I've been right. But I take small comfort from that. I shouldn't care to change places with you – for all your youth and beauty, my dear, for all your zest.'

'That sounds pretty bleak.'

'To be perfectly honest with you, if I didn't loathe taking pills so much, I'd cheerfully swallow a few too many and put an end to this miserable business of old age once and for all.'

'And you really *want* that?'

'It would be the sensible thing to do. It would be a kindness to your grandmother. With my dicky heart, you know, it's always been the understood thing that I would go first, but I'm afraid May is getting rather impatient.'

'What are these pills you're talking about, exactly,' Miranda said slowly, 'Valium, Mogadon, or is there something else?'

'Some kind of medical muck. Sleeping pills.'

'And you have a bad gag reaction?'

'What does that mean?'

'You have difficulty in swallowing them?'

'I'd sooner eat half a pound of your grandmother's bran.'

'I see. Well, you could quite easily mush them up in a glass of warm milk, you know, and –'

'I loathe warm milk.'

'Whisky then – which would be better actually. The alcohol would act to accelerate the central depressant effect.'

'What does all that mean?'

'It means it would be quicker.'

'Ummm.' He pursed his lips.

'I could give you a hand, if you like.'

'You could, could you?' He stared at her without blinking, then slowly shook his head. 'No, I don't think so.' He drew the skirts of the eiderdown closer about him. 'I'll take my own medicine when the time comes, thank you very much.'

'All right.' Miranda switched on the bedside lamp. 'Now, where do I find the haircutting stuff?'

Downstairs in the sitting room they drank their tea in silence.

May had taken out her knitting, but had not yet begun on it. The hot-water bottle covered by the shawl made a strange hump over her knees.

Rupert had made up the fire but not turned on the lights, and in the half darkness it was hard to tell whether or not May was asleep. He was careful to make no noise as he refilled his cup from the trolley. He had crept upstairs and changed, but all his clothes were the same – stout shoes, flannels, tweed jacket and tie, the prep schoolmaster's old-fashioned uniform. Milly would say he was as old-fashioned as the clothes – and perhaps she was right. He felt uneasy with age here. Time had gone wrong – stood still or moved too briskly, leaving the wrack of youth in a middle-aged man's carcase, making precocious children of the old, and the children wily with maturity.

He got up and took a taper from the mantelpiece and dipped it in the fire and lit his cigarette. He had managed to buy twenty in Richmond when Milly wasn't looking, but had forgotten the matches. But a cigarette was not what he wanted . . . a drink perhaps? Day after day would pass in this house without differentiation, all spent 'fastened to this chair'. 'Teach us to something (what?), Lord – teach us to sit still.' But he'd never been good at sitting still – 'Dodger' Darley the boys had called him because he was forever bobbing up and down, from side to side. And yet he had stuck it out for fifteen years at Brighton.

He heard a distant door open and a burst of laughter from

upstairs. He bent and turned on Oliver's light. Milly, he reflected, had never liked Brighton.

May gave a sigh and looked up. 'Are you still there?'

He smiled. 'I'm here alright.' Rain sprinkled the window pane and he thought briefly of the Rainbow Lady.

'Hello Daddy, hello Granny – here I am.' Miranda came in carrying a bundle under her arm.

'Hello, Milly – have a cup of tea?'

'Tea – brilliant. And the crumpets?'

'Here, on the trivet – but leave some for Oliver.'

'What *is* all that paraphernalia you've got there?' asked May.

'Smock, towel, sheet, scissors and a razor. I'm going to cut Grandad's hair.' She put the bundle on the couch and helped herself to a crumpet.

'We generally do that in the bedroom,' May said dryly. 'But no matter. How is he?'

'A bit tired, but bearing up.' Miranda wiped butter from her chin. 'He had a mild angina attack and got in rather a tizzy because he dropped his tablets. He ought to take it easy for a bit.'

'I see.' May drew a slow sigh. 'Then I suppose I should put off breaking the news to him.'

'About hospital? I don't know, Granny. Perhaps it might be wiser to wait till tomorrow – after he's had a good night's sleep.'

May nodded and sighed again, but in a different way – with relief, Rupert realized. The steeliness of her glance seemed to soften perceptibly, and his heart went out to her.

'Never do today what you can put off till tomorrow,' he said lightly, handing Miranda her tea.

'That's always been your motto, hasn't it, Daddy? What beautiful cups, I haven't seen these before. What are they – Royal Worcester?'

'Worcester? Good gracious me, no. They're Limoges. Rupert brought them out, though I couldn't tell you why.'

'The point of having beautiful things is to use them.'

'So you say – but you don't have to do the washing and cleaning, do you?'

'There is that, I suppose,' said Rupert, cook, bottle washer and maid of all work for as long as he could remember. He caught Miranda's eye and grinned.

Mollified, May picked up her knitting – a half-finished sock of lemon yellow. 'Yes, we bought a complete set in Paris on our honeymoon – twelve of everything, all very proper. I didn't realize at the time Oliver disliked tea – he drank it so dutifully, you see, and we didn't have much money, but I so fell in love with the Limoges that we blew practically our last penny on it. We had to eat in some *very* cheap places for our last day or two.'

'Grandad can't have liked that,' Miranda said, taking another crumpet.

'Oh, he wasn't interested in food in those days. "If we could just swallow a few pills in the morning to keep us going," he used to say, "what a lot of trouble it would save." No, all he wanted to do was see the sights – dragged me from pillar to post, did he not! He'd only been to Paris once – on a weekend leave during the War – but he'd read it all up beforehand in the most meticulous manner. I thought I knew Paris rather well, but I was quite put in my place, I can tell you. I had been there three or four times before and had even taken a school party, but I found I was. . . .'

She was off, in full flow. It was extraordinary the animation Milly seemed to inject into the old people. It was a gift of character or perhaps of youth – or perhaps simply the knack of directing her whole attention to the speaker.

Rupert unrolled the bundle on the couch. Sylvia had the same facility – her mind boring like a searchlight amidst the surrounding darkness. But he was not invigorated by the beam of that tunnel vision – on the contrary, his wits were set askew so that he became bumbling and sententious. He laid the sheet on the carpet and put a straight-backed Queen Anne chair in the centre of it. He brought over the standard lamp and switched it on. When intellectual passion marched in at the front door, humanity fled out the back.

'. . . though he always brought her back a hat in the latest Paris fashion, not that I recollect her ever wearing one. This particular time he took me along to the hat shop with him and insisted on trying on the hats himself. "*J'ai la même tête que ma femme*," I remember him saying airily as the shopgirls giggled – and he pranced about in front of the mirrors, dressed in his clerical garb of course. I suppose I'd laugh now, but then I wished the floor would open and swallow me up. It was the only time my father ever embarrassed me. And when he died and I was cleaning out the Rectory attic, I found every one of those hats – spick and span in their band boxes, just as good as new.'

'What did you do with them?'

'I rather think I gave them to the Women's Institute.'

'Oh *Granny*!' Miranda cried in pure agony.

'Why, dear – would you have liked them?'

'*Liked* them!' She groaned dramatically and then, as May and Rupert laughed, she glanced down at her old shirt and jeans and blushed. 'I don't *always* dress like this, you know.'

'Don't you, my dear?'

'You see – I'll wear a dress tomorrow!'

'That *will* be a treat,' said May mildly.

Miranda's clear laughter rang out. 'And you put on a new tie, old Poopa – that one's been mopping up the gravy far too long.'

'Righto,' said Rupert.

'That was most satisfactory,' Oliver said, swallowing the last morsel of the final crumpet. 'Now, my dear, I am quite ready.' He sat up straight in pyjamas and dressing gown he had put on for the ceremony.

'How do you like it?' Miranda asked, slipping the smock over his head.

'Short as you can make it.'

May said, 'He likes to look like a Prussian officer, don't you?'

'I do not like to look like a Prussian officer. It's merely that I detest a lot of loose foliage hanging over my ears. Alright – fire away. Rupert, it must be almost time for a drink.'

'Not just after all those crumpets!' Rupert said.

'Why not? – helps the digestion.'

'I expect he just wants "one for the road",' said May.

'It's not a. . . .' But Oliver's snappish reply was cut off as Miranda brusquely tilted his head forward and clicked the scissors.

'One for the road,' Rupert repeated thoughtfully. He lit another cigarette with the taper, then stood with his back to the fire. 'Reminds me of that theory of John McNulty's about resonant phrases. He –'

'John who?' said Oliver, head bowed.

'McNulty. He was –'

'Never heard of him.'

'What does it matter whether you've heard of him or not?' asked May sharply.

'It doesn't matter in the slightest, my dear. There are a great many people I've never heard of, and I don't suppose they're much the worse off for it. What was this McNutty's theory then, Rupert?'

'McNulty – he was a *New Yorker* writer in the thirties and a very brilliant one – died of drink, sadly enough.'

'Why "sadly"? I thought all *New Yorker* writers died of drink – nothing sad about it. Damned good way to go.'

'Oliver, why don't you just let Rupert get on with it?'

'Alright, my dear, alright. Anyway, he sounds like a good chap.'

'Head up, Grandad!' Miranda ran her hand down the nape of his neck. 'Now what am I going to do about all this baby fluff?'

'Some baby,' murmured May.

'Shave it off, I think. Daddy, hand me that hot water jug from the trolley.'

'Here we are. It's only tepid by now.'

'I should damn well hope so,' said Oliver.

'Come on, Daddy,' said Miranda, testing the razor against her thumb. 'I want to hear about this theory of yours.'

'It's not my theory, you know.'

'Never believed in theories,' Oliver said. Miranda began to giggle.

Rupert smiled. 'Anyway, the idea is that there are certain

words or phrases that are capable of summing up – well, all that the heart could desire. The trick is to repeat them over and over again, slowly – like an incantation – so that they gradually lull you into a kind of dreamlike enchantment, if you see what I mean.'

'No,' said Oliver, 'I don't.'

May paused in her knitting. 'Give us an example, Rupert.'

'I think one of them was "summer afternoon".'

'Summer afternoon?' May said, as though proffering an obscure crossword puzzle clue.

'Yes, but not like that. You have to murmur it slowly – languorously – over and over again. Now come on. Summer afternoon . . . summer afternoon. . . .'

'Summer afternoon, summer afternoon,' Oliver said in gravedigger tones.

'Summer afternoon,' May repeated crisply, as if ordering meat from a recalcitrant butcher, 'summer afternoon.'

'Summer afternoon summer after. . . .' Miranda was overcome by her giggles.

'No no.' Rupert laughed. 'Not like that. How can I explain?'

'Do you mean something like *carpe diem*?' said May. 'I always think *carpe diem* is –'

'I fancy that's more of a maxim.'

'Oh is it? I'm afraid I've never really understood the difference between maxims and mottoes and whatever those other things are called.'

'A picture of health?' said Miranda, recovering herself a little.

'That's better, Milly, much better, although –'

'A thousand guineas,' said Oliver.

'Ah, you're on the right track now.'

'Not that a thousand guineas would buy more than a couple of pairs of shoelaces these days.'

'Money doesn't really come into it.'

May said, 'A glass of champagne?'

'That's more like it. Terrific! Glass of champagne – glass of champagne. What could be more desirable than a glass of champagne?'

'Almost anything. Detestable muck!'

'Alright then, how about this? A month in the country . . . a month in the country . . . a month in the country,' said Rupert, half closing his eyes and swaying languidly.

'Which month – what country? If you'd been in England in February, my boy, instead of arsing about all over Islay, you'd have wished yourself almost anywhere else on the face of God's earth.'

'Try this one then,' said Rupert. 'The first day of Spring – that ought to gladden your heart. The first day of –'

'Make up your mind,' Oliver said testily, 'you told me the first day of Spring wasn't until tomorrow.'

'No, tomorrow's the last day of winter. I say, that's even better, isn't it? The last day of winter. Now come on, everybody, do make an effort!'

'The last day of winter . . . the last day of winter,' they all chanted together, 'the last day of winter.' But somehow the expected magic failed to materialize.

It was May who put an end to it. 'If you don't mind my saying so, Rupert, I prefer "the first day of spring". Lady Day, as we used to call it.'

'Lady Day?' said Miranda, carefully shaving the back of Oliver's neck. 'I thought that was something they did at Eton and Harrow.'

'No, dear,' said May, ignoring the spurt of male laughter, 'it's the Annunciation of the Virgin Mary. In olden times it used to be New Year's Day.'

Oliver tugged at the towel round his neck. 'You're muddling up the old New Year with the Vernal Equinox, which are not the same thing at all. Miranda, do you mind not pulling on this towel – it's throttling me.'

'Sorry, Grandad.'

'The way you're carrying on, it's a wonder she doesn't slit your throat,' May said tartly.

'That's not how it's done these days,' Oliver said. 'Pills and whisky is the modern method, eh, Miranda?'

'What *are* you talking about?' Rupert said.

'Let it pass, let it pass. Rupert, I've got a phrase for you which sums it all up pretty pithily, I think.'

'Oh yes,' said Rupert, with a vague feeling that he'd missed something important, 'what?'

'Fatal Heart Attack – repeat that one often enough and you'll soon be in another world.'

'And we know which one it will be in your case, don't we?' said May.

The tick of the old clock seemed suddenly louder; 'I told you so – I've seen it all,' it said primly into the silence.

'Well, there you are, Grandad, that's the best I can do.'

'Thank you, my dear, I'm most grateful. I feel years younger already.'

Miranda went round to inspect him from the front. 'Would you like me to shave you as well?'

'Shave me? Good Lord, I haven't been shaved for years. I should very . . . wait a minute, have you ever shaved anyone?'

'Oh yes – just a few weeks ago as a matter of fact, in pathology.'

'Pathology?'

May said, 'She means she shaved a corpse, don't you, my dear?'

'Yes, but it doesn't make any difference, the hair –'

'It damned well makes a difference to me! I don't fancy – *oooh*!' Oliver let out a loud groan and clutched the sides of the chair. 'Oooh – ooooh!'

Miranda knelt down and took hold of his wrist as Rupert crossed to her side.

'What is it? What's the matter? Is it his heart?'

Oliver writhed feebly, letting out animal bellows.

'I haven't the faintest.' Miranda frowned. 'His pulse rate's fine.'

'I think you'll find it's his cramps,' May said, glancing up from her knitting. 'In the legs – it usually takes him in the calf.'

Miranda immediately rolled up a pyjama leg and began kneading the calf.

'Other – leg,' Oliver gasped. 'Oooh . . . Jesus Christ!'

'I don't think Jesus Christ is going to be of much help to you just at the moment,' May said, as Miranda vigorously attacked the other leg.

'Aaaah!' he cried, struggling to rise, then falling back. 'Oh my God!'

'Don't talk,' Miranda said in a cool medical voice, 'just try and relax.'

'Re-ugh-lax! Good God-ugh-woman, how can I – ugh – relax – oooh!'

'What a good thing you're here,' May said, 'I can never do anything for him.'

'Is it better now, Grandad?'

'Yes. Oooh. Don't stop.'

'He has anti-cramp pills, but he won't take them of course. My mother always used to put camphor in the bed against cramp. Not that I think it ever did anything – except make the sheets smell rather disagreeable.'

Rupert said, 'I think you need a drink.'

'I do indeed, my boy. A large – ah – Grouse, if you wouldn't mind.'

'Enough?' said Miranda.

'I think so. Thank you, my dear. God bless you all, I feel myself again – as Sir Walter Scott is reputed to have remarked on his deathbed.'

'Well, you won't die of the cramps.' Miranda got to her feet. 'Not unless you were caught swimming.'

'That is a most unlikely eventuality. Ah, thank you, my boy,' Oliver said, accepting a rummer full of whisky. 'I can't swim.'

Rupert laughed. In the smock, with his pyjama legs rolled and his head cropped, the old man looked like an enormous Victorian baby at the seaside.

'Nor for that matter can I ride a bicycle,' Oliver said, taking a large swallow of whisky, 'or a horse.'

May said, 'And you're not even much good at hammering in a nail, are you, dear?'

'The only nails I expect to have hammered in are on my coffin – and I shall hardly be required to do that myself.'

'I think it's time we changed the subject,' May said. 'Miranda, my dear, if it isn't too much trouble, I am going to ask you to see to the supper tonight.'

'Of course I will, Granny – what are we having?'

She lifted the smock over Oliver's head and whisked the clothes brush round the inside of his collar.

'I don't mind doing it,' said Rupert, pouring himself a drink.

'I'm not asking you, I'm asking Miranda. Now, my dear, do you know how to make a cauliflower cheese?'

'Oh, I should think so.'

'Well, if nobody objects,' Oliver said, finishing his whisky and struggling to his feet, 'I am going to bed. All this business has rather taken it out of me.'

'What, without any supper?' Miranda asked, astonished.

'I've no doubt I could be prevailed upon to partake of a small portion, if one of you young people brought it up to me.' He limped slowly to the door. 'And I wouldn't say no to a glass of Burgundy to go with it – purely for medicinal purposes of course.'

'Well,' said May when the door had shut behind him, 'it's a most extraordinary thing how when you don't particularly want him in the room, he hangs about like a bad penny, and when you do want him to sit still for half an hour, off he immediately scuttles.'

Rupert smiled. 'Like Cumming who was always going, and Gowing who was always coming.'

'Is it? Now come and sit down on the poufe, Miranda, and tell me – have you ever made a cauliflower cheese before?'

'No, not exactly.'

'It's not very difficult,' Rupert said, coming to stand in front of the fire with his glass. 'She's watched me do it dozens of times, haven't you, Milly?'

'Have I? I expect I have.'

'I'm not addressing you, Rupert. Now, to start with, do you know how to make a *sauce Mornay*?'

'No, I'm afraid not.'

'Don't worry,' Rupert said, 'it's just a fancy name for a cheese sauce.'

'Tsch!' May put down her knitting. 'I see I shall have to do something about your culinary education. I'm afraid you ought to be rather ashamed of yourself. At least you know what a *béchamel* is?'

'I'm sorry, Granny, I don't think I do.'

'Well I'll be blowed!'

'It's just an ordinary white sauce.' Rupert sipped his malt. 'The thing you've got to watch out for is that the milk's not too hot, otherwise –'

'And who asked you?' said May.

'Do I have to be asked?' He smiled lightly. 'I thought this was a general conversation.'

'And what gave you that idea? I happen to be talking to Miranda. If all you can do is interrupt, I suggest you leave the room.'

'Leave the. . . .' His smile died under her unwavering gaze. Ridiculously, he felt himself blushing. 'Alright,' he said, 'if that's what you –'

'Go on then – be off with you!'

'Daddy!' Miranda half rose but was waved down by May.

Rupert walked to the door, carefully carrying his glass, although his hand shook slightly.

'Granny,' said Miranda as he went out, 'I think –'

'Just like his father – always interrupting. Well, now we can get on with it. I think you'd better note this down. You'll need pencil and paper and. . . .'

Rupert put his glass on the hallstand and took the keys from the brass box and set about unlocking the front door. The trembling in his fingers made him clumsy and the bolts were stiff, but he got it open at last. He took a shaky breath – he felt absurdly edgy and weak with effort. He leant against the doorway and his elbow touched off the bell. Rupert flinched away.

'Damn,' he muttered. He took out a cigarette and patted his pockets in search of matches.

'Was that you ringing the bell?'

Rupert jumped and, turning, saw Oliver at the end of the hall by his studio door.

'Sorry,' he said. 'Mistake – just trying to get out.'

'Were you indeed?' Oliver said, amused. 'Well, whether you're going or staying, I suggest you shut the door – there's an Arctic breeze whistling about my ankles.'

'Right – sorry.' Rupert stepped back into the hall and shut the door. 'You wouldn't happen to have a match?'

'In pyjamas? Hardly. But come along in – there are plenty of matches in here.'

The studio was dim and warm, lit only by the small lamp over the drafting board and the glow of the gas fire.

'I am having some bread and butter,' Oliver said, picking up a slice from a plate on the desk. 'The new bread Vi brought this morning – would you care for some?'

'No thanks – just a match.'

'On the mantelpiece,' said Oliver and watched attentively as Rupert lit his cigarette with shaky hand. 'What's up?'

'Oh, nothing really.' Rupert managed a smile. 'May just sent me out of the room.'

'Hell's teeth – why does that sort of thing always have to happen when I'm not there? What for?'

'I thought she was getting at Milly a bit, so I chipped in and –'

'– and got your head snapped off. Well, I'm sorry, my boy – but I'm sure Miranda can look after herself.'

'Yes, but you know how it is – May can get so frightfully fierce.'

'Oh don't I know it, don't I know it.' He ate the last crust and wiped his buttery fingers on the seat of his dressing gown. 'She can be as sharp as ever she was – sharper perhaps.' He perched himself on the drafting stool. 'But she doesn't mean it. We're getting old – and the old often become selfish and inconsiderate. All these aches and complaints – the whole structure crumbling. It makes us self-absorbed and petulant, I'm afraid – I am myself.

Sometimes I hear myself talking and I say, you silly old bugger, you're the sort of chap I used to be rude to on principle when I was younger. But most of the time, you see, you *don't* hear yourself spouting all this nonsense, repeating yourself, telling the same old story over and over and over again. And even if you did, you wouldn't know it half the time – because the memory's going.

'That's the trouble with your mother of course – memory. Sometimes I tell her something for the fourth or fifth time – like a dentist's appointment, for instance – and she says, why didn't you tell me before? So I say, I'm most frightfully sorry, my dear, I thought I had – I'm afraid my memory isn't as good as it was. Of course there's nothing on earth the matter with my memory, but it makes her feel better, you see – or I think it does. Losing your memory is losing touch with the world – and it's hard to accept that as your own fault – which is why your mother spends so much time with her blasted wireless, of course.' His tone was as mild and light as the music with which he had once filled the house.

'But you're not really out of touch, Oliver,' Rupert said, the ash of his cigarette falling unnoticed to the floor.

'Oh but I am – oh yes I am.' He gave his faintly lopsided smile. 'But I *have* still got my memory – not for personal things, but I regard that of not of the slightest significance – for what I've built, for what I've read, for what I've done. And I can come in here and forget about all the rest of it.' With a broad sweep of the hand he dismissed the house, the night, London, the remainder of the unquiet world.

'In the old days I always used to go up to the Club – but the pins are not up to it anymore. Of course, I could always hire a car, if I could afford it – which I can't. And to tell you the truth, the last two or three times I went up in a car, I found the traffic quite terrifying. No, I shan't venture in a motor car again, I'm resigned to that – the stairlift will be about as much as I can manage. No, I am quite happy at home – quite happy – and lots of people come to see me, you know. Too many in fact. But tell me, what's London like these days? How's the Club?'

'The Club?' Rupert found an ashtray amidst the clutter on the desk and stubbed out his cigarette; as he did so, he noticed the drawing taped to the bookcase. 'Oh,' he said, looking back at Oliver, 'it seems to be filled with men one doesn't know – though quite a few people come up to me and ask after you. Which reminds me, somebody called West wanted to be remembered to you.'

'West? An absolute four-letter man! Why he should imagine I want to remember him, I can't think. I'd rather remember an unwiped bottom.'

Rupert smiled and for a moment his gaze returned to the drawing. 'And then there was Inskilling – you do recall Inskilling?'

'Very well. And I may say I was extremely fond of Ray Inskilling at one time. Brilliant in his way, you know, absolutely brilliant – but always a teeny-weeny bit unsound, and he got religion in his old age. In fact he wrote to me not so long ago asking whether he mightn't send me a little book of meditations he'd put out.'

'How very interesting.'

'Interesting?'

'Well, wasn't it?'

'I haven't the faintest idea. I wrote back and said he most certainly might *not* send me any such thing. Meditations? At my age! What in God's name for?'

Rupert laughed. 'That must have been a bit of a blow for him.'

'Well then he can damn well meditate about that.' And, having shot his bolt, he laughed too. 'Now I'm off to bed.' He got to his feet and, collecting the empty bread and butter plate, made his way to the door. 'Turn off the gas fire, will you, there's a good chap? No, not that way – the other way. That's right. And the light.'

Rupert paused with his hand over the lamp. 'Oliver – is that the Pyramid?' He gestured to the drawing on the wall.

'Yes, that's it. Old Maybury came in and lent me a hand putting it up. Come along.'

Rupert switched off the light and followed Oliver into the hall, shutting the door behind him.

'I'm afraid it's very boring looking at people you don't know and never will – even if they are your ancestors.' May smiled and closed the photograph album and put in on the table.

'Oh no, it's very interesting really,' Miranda said, resisting a yawn.

'As a matter of fact I do have something that might interest you – something rather special.' May opened her Tunbridgeware box, removed the inner tray and took out a flat parcel wrapped in tissue paper. 'We didn't call them "shots" – or even snaps. You had to sit still for quite two or three minutes without so much as a twitch of the eyelid.' She undid the wrapping and removed a photographic plate. 'Here you are – take it by the edges, that's right. Now you have to hold it up to the light.'

Miranda crossed to the other side of the fireplace and held the plate over Oliver's reading lamp.

'My father took it, of course. Photography was a great hobby of his, and I believe he was one of the very first people to make his own colour plates – or so they tell me.'

'Why, Granny, it's brilliant.' Miranda glanced from the plate to May and back again. 'How beautiful you were – I mean –'

'Oh don't mind me, my dear, I know I'm not much to look at these days.'

'It's not that, it's just that. . . .' She looked at May with wonder.

'I was certainly pretty. Of course Dad took it in profile, which was clever of him because my nose was always my best feature.' Unconsciously she raised her head. 'We had quite a time of it – it took half the afternoon before he got it right. He chose the colours with the utmost care – a pink sash at the waist and a pink ribbon round my new hat, and my new white summer dress and I had to be holding cornflowers, to go with my eyes. It was August, you know, and I'd just finished my last year at the Ladies College and life was all before me. Oh I was very full of myself.'

Miranda came back slowly and sat down and, leaning over, took May's hand.

'Would you care to have it, my dear?'

'Could I – could I really?'

'Take it with my blessing.' She patted Miranda's hand. 'It will serve as a reminder of what we once were – and what we all come to in the end.'

Rupert sat on the bed in his dressing gown, waiting for the hot water bottle to take the chill off the sheets. He was tired, but he knew he would have a sleepless night – although it was not yet eleven, Oliver had already been to the bathroom twice and each time the ancient water tank groaned and clanked like the pulling up of a drawbridge. But on a normal night that would not have kept him awake. The normality here was not his – and it was that which disturbed him. The house was heavy with intimations of decay, of slack breath uneasily drawn, brief dreams, the detritus of all desire.

At May's request he had wound the longcase clock for the coming week. It had seemed to him that the weights were reluctant to be dragged into position, and that the shrillness of the chime and the irritability of the tick were protests against a duty that marked a time indifferent to the processes of nature, where all was change.

'Come in,' he said to a knock on the bedroom door. 'Oh, hello, Milly.'

Miranda, dressed only in cotton pyjamas, shivered. 'It's glacial in here, Daddy – why don't you turn on the fire?'

'It keeps backfiring with a noise like a machine gun. I don't think it's been lit for years.'

'You must be chilled to the bone. I've made some cocoa, do you want some?'

'I wouldn't say no.'

'Come along then. It's in my room – or your room, rather.'

They went silently along the darkened passage – a light might have disturbed the old people who kept their bedroom door permanently ajar (a measure taken originally in case of childish nightmare, then as a precaution against burglars, now simply a venerable usage).

'This is a bit better,' Rupert said, taking the old easy chair. 'I sometimes think this is the most comfortable room in the house.'

'That wouldn't be hard,' Miranda said, passing him a mug of cocoa, but she said it smiling.

'I suppose not.' He looked round happily at the bubbling gas fire, Milly's neatly arranged clothes, a couple of medical textbooks on the mantelpiece – *Elements of Psychiatry for Medical Students* and one simply entitled *Accidents* – and the portrait of himself as a boy.

'Who took that?'

'Grandfather – May's father. I must have been five or six – no, five, I think. Anyway, it was the year I spent with the grandparents when Oliver and May went off to Germany and various places.'

'You must have hated it.'

'Hated it? On the contrary, it was one of the happiest years of my life. Oh I see, you're thinking of May's mother – but Granny wasn't a bit like *they* say, you know. At least, not to me. She was always sweetness itself to me – she used to tell me the most marvellous stories and she had a beautiful singing voice even in her old age. You know, she could repeat whole chunks of Dickens by heart? And he was the most unlikely clergyman you could imagine. It seemed to me he could explain anything – from the internal combustion engine to sunspots. He tutored me – I didn't have to go to school – and that's largely how I caught up after the disastrous time at the Steiner school. He taught me all sorts of things – chess and croquet and bridge, even billiards.' He sipped the cocoa.

'That's a really terrific shot of you. Where was it?'

'Let's see – Bognor, I believe. Or was it Lyme Regis? I'd had rather a bad go of measles and the doctor recommended a week at the seaside. We stayed in one of those magnificent old hotels full of potted palms and wicker work furniture – and tremendous amounts of food. And every day we went to the beach. January or February, it must have been, I think – at any rate we had the hotel almost to ourselves, and were consequently treated like royalty. Or so I thought.'

'Yes,' said Miranda, 'you do look pretty pleased with yourself.'

Rupert laughed, though he would not have put it quite that way. The boy was grinning, yes, but the stance was proud and passionate, triumphal almost.

'Daddy?'

'Yes?'

'What are you going to do with yourself?'

'Do with myself?'

'Well, where are you going to live, for one thing?'

'I don't know – I rather thought I might go abroad.'

'Abroad!' Miranda sat cross-legged on the bed. She looked down at her cocoa and slowly removed the skin with the tip of her finger. 'You know – you could always come and – and live with me for a bit. There is a spare room in the flat – of course it's a bit primitive. . . .'

'That wouldn't worry me. Thank you, Milly. But somehow I don't really think. . . .'

'No. I thought you wouldn't.' She looked straight at him. 'You've had too much of women, haven't you, poor old thing?'

'I wouldn't quite say that, but –'

'Oh wouldn't you? Then I was right. You do fancy her.'

'Who?'

'Mrs smarmy Hamilton.'

He smiled. 'Oh come on, Milly – I hardly know the woman.'

'I don't mean *her* particularly. Any woman.'

He thought fleetingly of the woman in the train, shook his head. 'Not in any real sense. . . . The boot's rather on the other foot – I wouldn't want to cramp your style. I'm a bit of a middle-aged bore. I don't think I'd go down too well with your friends. . . .'

'I suppose you mean Archie. You don't like him, do you?'

Rupert hesitated, then said truthfully, 'No, not much.'

'Why? Because he's a drop-out?'

'No. I suppose it's instinctive. I've got nothing against drop-outs, you know. After all, in one sense or another, I've been a drop-out myself most of my life – at least, until I took up school-mastering.'

'And now you are again.' Miranda had a furry brown moustache on her upper lip from the cocoa. 'And it really doesn't bother you, does it?'

'No,' he said, surprised at her perception. 'In fact, in an odd way, it's a relief.' He finished the cocoa and put the mug on the floor. He glanced up at the boy on the beach and hesitated – but her silence encouraged him.

'I nearly dropped out for good and all once.' He paused, but she still said nothing. 'It was just before we moved to Brighton – in the old house. It was early one summer morning and I'd gone out into the garden before breakfast. The sun shone but there was still dew on the ground and I was standing there drinking my cup of tea when suddenly I became aware of some change – an alteration in the air, the atmosphere. I don't know – it's almost impossible to describe. But I seemed to see and hear and feel each daisy on the lawn, each separate blade of grass, every leaf – the insects, the butterflies, even the worms under the earth . . . all vibrant with a kind of life magnified, oh, a thousand times in intensity – outside time, transcendent. And I was a part of it – though not yet fully *of* it. Trembling on the brink, you might say. The walls were down, the door was open and there was a life there of – of ineffable exaltation. I knew that all I had to do was to take one step – and it would be mine. . . .'

'Then why didn't you?' Miranda said after a silence.

'Oh – practical difficulties.' He smiled, brought to himself. 'It would have meant giving up everything – you, Mum, the house we'd just brought, the job I'd just got, all ordinary life, all normal attachments. . . . Everyone would have thought I was going mad, and perhaps after all, it was a delusion. I was quite unworthy to receive such a – a flood of grace. And then. . . .'

'Yes?'

'Well, I don't know, perhaps I used it as an excuse, but I remembered something John Crowe Ransom had written. I can't recall the exact words, but it was something to the effect that the man who aspires to pure goodness – or saintliness – limits himself, no longer possesses the entire vitality which Providence had intended for him – he has not chosen the whole joy of life. It's a Manichaean argument of course, but it seems to me to have a certain validity.'

'So you became a schoolmaster instead.'

'So I became a schoolmaster instead.'

'But you still want to go back and find your – your vision, is that it?'

'Good heavens, there's no going back! You only get one chance like that in a lifetime, and if you don't take it – well, you have to make do with what you've got.'

Miranda sighed. Then, frowning, she said, 'But you've not even got unemployment.'

Rupert put back his head and laughed aloud.

'What's so funny?'

'I'm sorry, Milly. It's just that . . . well, don't you worry about me.'

'But what are you going to *do*?' She leant forward almost angrily.

'As a matter of fact, I had a letter from a producer the other day – he might be interested in making a musical out of *Aftertaste*. Of course it probably won't come to anything, but it would be amusing if it did.'

'Amusing,' she said, neutrally testing the word. 'But wouldn't that be going back?'

'I suppose it would in a way,' he said with a smile. 'I'm afraid you've got me there. But it would be new to me in a way – I'd like to try my hand at writing lyrics.'

'I see.'

'Perhaps I should be pushing off.'

'No, don't go yet, Daddy.' She put down her mug and hitched her feet under her more comfortably. Rupert kept quiet, sensing her awkwardness.

'I nearly dropped out once too,' she said abruptly, 'from med. school, I mean.'

'I didn't know. When was that?'

'Early on. It was a week or two before I was due to go up for my second year and I was, well, what Granny would call "full of myself". It was that time I went to Cornwall with Johnny Landis and his sister and her boyfriend. They weren't medical students of course, and I expect I was showing off a bit. We came to this wood – more of a little copse really – in a valley, and Johnny insisted on poking about in it, although it looked rather dark and nasty, particularly as it was a lovely sunny day outside. After a minute or two, Johnny started calling me in that sort of panicky way that puts your heart in your mouth. He'd found an abandoned car – heaven knows how it had got there – and there was a man lying on the back seat. "I think he's dying," Johnny said. So without really thinking, I got in the back of the car and started giving him the kiss of life. And then after a minute or two, I touched his hand – it was stone cold and slightly slimy. Then I got my head together and looked properly and of course he was dead – and had been dead quite a long time, two weeks at least it turned out eventually.' She shivered. 'I've never felt such a fool in my whole life. He was rotting, Daddy.'

'My God, you poor kid.' He stretched out a hand to comfort her, but she shook her head.

'Poor idiot was nearer the truth. There I was with my first real emergency – only it wasn't of course, which only made it worse – and I forgot everything I knew and just panicked.'

'So you thought you'd never be any good?'

'Yes, but it was more than that somehow, more than just injured pride. I felt . . . frightened.' She looked down at her hands in her lap.

And Rupert knew that she was looking at the face of the old man in the back of the car – old man, why old? He might have been any age, anyone, husband, father, brother, son. . . . 'Who was the man?' he asked.

She raised her head. 'I. . . .' She shook her head and bit her lip. 'They never found out – he had no identification. A tramp, they thought.'

'I see.' He paused. 'But you didn't quit, all the same.'

'No,' she said quickly, 'I worked like a dog instead. And it made me decide what I was going to specialize in, if I got the chance.'

'You've never told me – I thought you were aiming to be a GP.'

'Never! Accidents, that's what I'm specializing in.'

'Accidents? Is that a specialization? What, motor accidents?'

'Any kind of accident. It's newish, but not that new. Motor accidents are part of it of course – at places like Birmingham probably the main part. But it includes any emergency from third-degree burns to respiratory heart failure. At Addenbrookes, for example, there are a lot of agricultural accidents – mangled feet, severed limbs, crushed ribs. That can mean getting into micro-surgery. There's terrific variety. And there's something you can do about it right there and then – something you've got to do about it.'

'It sounds – exciting.'

'It *is* exciting. It – oh Daddy, you're squeamish!' She laughed.

'I'm afraid I am a bit – am I turning blue about the gills?' He smiled, but he could feel the cocoa agitating. He closed his eyes, which was a mistake because he immediately saw crushed feet and mangled stumps of arms – all the ghastly bloodiness he had just missed in the war.

'Come on, I'd better put you to bed.'

'No no, I'm alright.' He opened his eyes and stood up. 'Don't you worry, we're not lost,' he said, repeating the chorus line of one of the first stories he'd ever told her.

He bent down and kissed her cheek. 'Goodnight.'

'Goodnight.'

He opened the door and stepped out into the passage.

'Poopa,' she said softly.

He turned his head. 'Yes – what is it?'

'I'm glad you've left Mum,' she whispered.

In the bedroom, May turned the page of *The New Testament in Large Type*:

> Therefore when thou doest thine alms, do not sound a trumpet before thee, as the hypocrites do in the synagogues and in the streets, that they may have glory of men. . . .

She looked up and listened to the small noise of the rain on the window. Laying down the book, she took two pills from the bottle and swallowed them with a glass of water.

She picked up the book and read on:

> . . . when thou doest alms, let not thy left hand know what thy right hand doeth, that thine alms may be in secret. . . .

In the other bed, the old man stirred. 'Aluminium,' he said in a clear voice, 'aluminium . . . aluminium.'

May waited, but he had said what he had to say and fell quiet again. In a little while she took off her glasses and turned out the light.

3

Sunday

'Do you trust me, Granny, after last night?' Miranda grinned. She had fulfilled her promise and wore an ivory-coloured knit dress with a wide leather belt.

'My dear, I'm sure your cauliflower cheese was very tasty – Rupert thought so, didn't you, Rupert?'

'First rate.'

'And the steak and kidney pie is made, so all you have to do is heat it up – and make the roast potatoes.'

'I'll give you a hand with that,' Rupert said, 'if I'm allowed to, that is.'

'I think you've learned your lesson.' May gave him a little nod. 'Just remember that Oliver likes them rather overdone.' She glanced at the ceiling. 'It's almost half past eleven – what is he doing up there?'

'Poshing himself up,' said Miranda. 'I caught a glimpse of him tying his bow tie as I came down. And he was singing in the bathroom – that's a good sign, isn't it?'

'As long as it wasn't "Lead Kindly Light" – that always means he's depressed. The Encircling Gloom, you know.' May sat with her hands in her lap – no knitting or sewing this morning.

Rupert moved restlessly about the room – earlier he had made up the fire and dusted and swept, plumped up the cushions and changed the water in the flower vases. Now there was nothing to do but wait. It was not just the waiting that was oppressive, but a latent feeling of deceit that sat on them all – all innocent, the old man would be walking into a sort of emotional ambush. And it was totally unnecessary. Any doctor worth his salt would have told him right away on the spot, at the same time he'd made the hospital recommendation to May. But Rupert remembered Dr Bowson – a tall tallow-candle of a man who took refuge behind a dignified manner and a lugubrious countenance. Now, if Milly had been in charge. . . . He glanced at her, sitting on the pink couch as patiently as May in her chair, and with something of the same delicate strength of feature – but would not she have been *too* brisk perhaps? Accidents – that would call for nerve and resource and decisiveness; no time for the more refined virtues of the healer. On the other hand. . . .

'Hark!' said May at the sound of a thump on the stairs.

'Christ Al-bloody-mighty!'

'I think that must be him,' said Miranda – and even May smiled.

'May,' Oliver said, throwing open the door, 'I nearly broke my neck on those bloodstained stairs – one of the runners has come loose.'

'We'll ask Rupert to fix it,' May said calmly.

'I've already fixed it. That's not the point.' He gave a tug at his waistcoat and glared at them all. He too had dressed up for the Sabbath – dove-grey pinstripe suit, with waistcoat, bow tie and all the accoutrements in canary yellow.

'Good morning, Grandad.'

'Morning. Rupert, come here a moment, would you.' He turned to the window. 'Look – you see those men?'

'Where?'

'There by the gate – those scruffy-looking individuals. I've been watching them from the upstairs window – they've been hanging about for half an hour.'

'Half an hour?'

'Five or ten minutes – they keep going away and coming back

again. I'd say they're up to a bit of no good, wouldn't you?'

'Casing the joint, you mean?'

'Precisely. I think we should call the police at once.'

'That's going overboard a bit, isn't it? They're probably just admiring the house. But why don't I go out and ask them what they're up to?'

'Would you? Well – alright. But you'd better take my shooting stick with you.'

'Wouldn't he be better off with your bedside sword?' said Miranda, who'd come to have a look too.

'It's no joking matter, my dear,' Oliver said severely, 'those ruffians might get up to anything. Besides, my sword is for ceremonial purposes only.'

May said, 'You once killed a mouse with it in the kitchen.'

'These chaps are *not* mice!'

'Well,' said Rupert, 'here goes.'

'I'll come too, Daddy.'

'Now, Miranda, I'd really rather you stayed here.'

'Don't worry, Grandad – safety in numbers, you know. If they start anything, I'll scream.'

'And who do you think will come to your rescue – old Maybury?'

'More likely to be Mrs Hamilton and her dog, don't you think so, Daddy?' said Miranda, catching up to Rupert as he wrestled with the front door.

'You shouldn't tease the old boy so,' he muttered.

'Nonsense – he loves it.'

Rupert swung the door open and stepped out. 'Good morning,' he called, advancing up the path, 'can I help you?'

'Oh dear, have we been disturbing you?' said the first man in vibrantly cultivated tones.

'Not me, but my father thought you might be prospective burglars.'

'Burglars! How lovely!' He laughed pleasantly, then immediately looked serious. 'I really am most terribly sorry. I say, may I come in?'

'Of course, of course.'

He pushed open the gate and stepped into the garden, looking keenly about him. He wore spectacles and an old navy blue duffle coat. 'I'm so glad you came out,' he said, 'we didn't want to come and knock on your door – it being Sunday and all that, you know.'

Miranda suddenly laughed.

'Oh dear, have I said something funny?' He managed to look distressed and interested at the same time. 'By the way, my name's Calder – Roy Calder. I'm a BBC producer, and this is my designer, Charles White.'

'Hi,' said White, a pale young man in a short-sleeved shirt with a camera round his neck.

'Hullo. I'm Rupert Darley, and this is my daughter Miranda.'

'Terrific!' Calder said with gusto. 'Well, look here, I expect you're wondering what all this is about? The fact is I'm producing a seventy-five minute teleplay – family comedy sort of thing, but with a bit of a different twist – and we're looking for an outside location for two or three days shooting. And I must say at first peep I think your house is just exactly what we want.'

'Well, it's my father's house, you know, not mine.'

'Oh.' Calder's face fell. 'And you think he might object?'

'Not necessarily – you'd have to ask him. What do you think, Milly?'

'I should think he'd object like fury – but I'm sure *you* could talk him round.'

'Do you think so?' Calder beamed at her with large white teeth. 'Of course we haven't seen the sides and the back yet, but I really think this is it – don't you, Charlie?'

'Yeah – fine.'

'Are you sure,' said Rupert dubiously, turning to look at the house. 'It looks rather on the shabby side, I'm afraid.'

'But, my dear fellow, that's *exactly* what we want. Look at the worn whitewash and the peeling shutters and the garden, yes, definitely getting out of hand a bit. Gentle decline and all that. Oh no – *splendidly* shabby, couldn't be better!' He had moved on up the path as he spoke. 'There isn't a summerhouse, by any chance?' he said, casting a quick sidelong glance at Miranda.

'There is, as a matter of fact,' Rupert said. 'I think it's probably adequately shabby.'

'Terrific! Otherwise we should have had to build one – not that that's really a problem.'

'In that case,' Miranda said blandly, 'why couldn't you have built the house too?'

'Ah, now that would be a bit of a problem. You see, Miranda – may I call you Miranda? You see, it's really a question of budget – and as there's only going to be about twelve actual minutes on film, it's hardly worth it. I say, Charlie, look at that dustbin behind the bay tree. Why is the lid chained on?'

'Is it?' said Rupert. 'So it is. I've no idea.'

'Burglars?' suggested Miranda.

'Burglars – terrific!' Calder laughed richly. 'Garlic and sapphires in the garbage.'

'Look,' said Rupert as the designer raised his camera, 'I really ought to ask my father before you start any of that.'

'Right. I'm terribly sorry. Shall we wait here?'

'Well, if you wouldn't mind.'

'Oh by the way – if we did decide to use the house, we would pay of course.'

'Oh – I'm glad you told me. That might make a difference.'

'Now, look here, under no conceivable circumstances will I tolerate a bunch of BBC homosexuals prancing about my house – let's get that straight.'

Rupert sighed. 'I'm quite sure they're not homosexual,' he said, looking out of the window to where Calder was writing on a piece of paper and tearing it in half and handing it to Miranda with much laughter. 'And it's my impression it's the outside of the house they're interested in, not the inside.'

'No. May – you wouldn't like a gang of half-tight trade unionists trampling about your garden, would you?'

'It's a matter of complete indifference to me. What do you

think they'd do – make faces at the window?'

'I still say –'

'They mentioned something about payment.'

'Payment?' Oliver shifted in his chair. 'How much?'

'I don't know.' How old was Calder – thirty-five? No, forty at least – that sort of rich public-school accent had died out in the under-forties. And so had that supreme confidence with which he was swiftly wooing Milly. 'You could always ask him.'

'Good idea. Have the fellow in and we'll pop the question. I expect it'll turn out to be twopence-halfpenny.'

'Oh Oliver – must we?' May said miserably.

'Don't worry – it won't take long. "How much?" "Sixpence." "Bugger off."'

'That's what you say now – but in five minutes you'll be offering them drinks and . . . and I rather wanted to talk to you.'

'You've got all day to talk to me, my dear – all year, come to that. Now, go on, my boy – what are you hanging about for?'

Rupert watched them from the front door for a moment, feeling almost as miserable as May.

'We'll have to shoot the front of the house over the hedge from the road,' Calder said, gesticulating grandly. 'That means a sizeable truck and a lot of equipment – is there normally much traffic on this road?'

'I shouldn't think so.'

'Marvellous! Not that it matters a lot – people never seem to mind being diverted if it's for TV. Magic words, you see. In fact, they usually stop and gawp – just as they do at motor accidents – and you know all about that of course.' He grinned. 'The big problem in this neighbourhood is –'

'Mr Calder!'

'Hallo!'

'I wonder if you'd come in for a minute or two and have a word with my father.'

'Love to. Do you mind if Charles here pokes about a bit meanwhile? I promise he won't lift the camera till you say the word.'

'Of course we don't mind,' Miranda said, leading Calder to the front door, 'do we, Daddy?'

Rupert shrugged and stepped aside.

'Give me your coat, Roy.'

'No really, I –'

'Oh come on, it's like a greenhouse in the sitting room.'

Without the duffle coat, Calder was revealed as surprisingly lean and muscular – surprising to Rupert, who had pictured him fattish and flabby.

'Well come in, come in.' Rupert opened the door and ushered them in. 'This is Mr Roy Calder,' he said as pompously as any butler. 'My father, Oliver Darley – and my mother.'

'How do you do,' said Calder, deferentially bending to May and taking her rather reluctant hand. 'Mrs Darley, I do apologize for barging in on you like this – on Sunday of all days, too.'

'We are not religious in this household, Mr Calder,' May said, but the severity was tinged with a hint of mollification. He had said the right thing; now he looked at her sympathetically and nodded slowly.

Masterly, thought Rupert, as Calder strode over to Oliver. 'Mr Darley – Darley? Oliver Darley – of course, the architect! How stupid of me to be so slow on the uptake. I *am* delighted.'

'Well, you'd better sit down,' said Oliver, not so easily taken in by this sort of thing. (Miranda, thought Rupert, had no doubt given Calder an encapsulated life history of the entire household in the five minutes they'd been together.) 'I understand from my son that you have a proposition to put to me.'

'Absolutely.' He sat down in the centre of the couch, started to speak, then paused and looked quickly round the room. 'I say, am I right – you haven't got a television set?'

'No,' Oliver said, 'we haven't.'

'You never watch?'

'No – never.'

'Terrific!'

Oliver grunted. 'Do I understand you to be denigrating your own *metier*, Mr Calder?'

'No no,' he answered eagerly, 'but every profession has its blinkers and television more than most. As an architect, sir, I'm sure you understand what it is to work in a *metier* where aesthetic excellence is constantly curbed not just by commercial necessity but also by pressures from the ignorant and opinionated.'

'I do indeed,' Oliver said, with a faintly amused smile.

'One simply isn't free to do what one wants to do – and even where you do do what you want to do, you can never do it exactly in the way you want to do it. I don't suppose there are more than a couple of dozen programmes a year that are really worth watching, if that.'

'I'm delighted to have my opinion confirmed. May, do you hear that? Mr Calder says television is no good. My wife is an inveterate listener in to the wireless.'

'Ah.' Calder turned to May. 'You listen a great deal? You enjoy it?'

'For some of us oldsters the radio is a lifeline, but I must say I find it a little odd for an ordinary person like me to be congratulated on not watching TV.'

'Ah, but you've hit on just the word, Mrs Darley – ordinary. If you were ordinary, which I very much doubt, watching television would only make you more ordinary – it would reduce you to a settled level of ordinariness which would then be used as a justification for making even more ordinary programmes. You wouldn't be talking in the way you do at all.'

'That sounds like a very elitist argument,' Miranda said suddenly. 'Surely something can be ordinary and good.'

'Of course it can – take, well, the Archers, for example. But –'

'The Archers – pooh!' May said. 'Such a tiresome lot – nothing but palaver and not a cupful of commonsense between them. Most *ex*traordinary.'

'You're joking!' said Calder with a delighted smile.

'Not at all. When I was a girl, we lived in a Norfolk rectory and I can tell you the country people were not remotely like those ridiculous Archer people.'

'Norfolk? Whereabouts in Norfolk?'

'Not far from Downham Market.'

'Good heavens – how extraordinary. Then you must have known my great uncle Gerald – he was archdeacon of Wisbech.'

'Gerald Calder – why, of course. He often used to come over for tennis. He had a very pretty daughter – Amelia – and a son, now what was his name?'

'Herbert. He was killed in the Western Desert.'

'And Amelia? Now something funny happened to her, didn't it?'

'She went into an Anglican convent – an enclosed order. She's still alive – my people go up to see her once a year. They say she's terrifically happy.'

'Look,' said Oliver restively, 'I hate to interrupt this family pow-wow, but do you think we could get down to business? What exactly is it that you want of us, Mr Calder?'

Rupert had moved over to the window that gave on to the garden at the back, from where he could watch with equal facility the antics of the designer outside and those of the producer inside. And, observing Calder going to work on the Darleys, he wondered that Milly had chosen for once the obvious charmer over the pale young man in the garden – a lame duck, if ever there was one (though possibly designers were all like that). She sat beside Calder on the couch, not foolishly entranced, but fascinated – as though he was an interesting case of a crushed knee or a mangled ear. Rupert shook his head abruptly and lit a cigarette. At least May was momentarily soothed.

'. . . and you can assure me that there will be no disturbance? We're not up to providing cups of tea for the workmen, you know.'

'No tea – I assure you.'

'Good. Then the only question remaining to be discussed is how much you are willing to pay.'

'Well, sir, it's not entirely up to me. But if we're counting on two and a half to three days, I would think certainly a thousand, possibly twelve hundred.'

'Twelve hundred pounds, eh?' Oliver stroked his chin. 'Well, my dear sir, I think something might be arranged on that basis.'

'Terrific – then I'll talk to my people and try to get back to you some time early next week, would that be alright?' Calder was on his feet.

'Quite satisfactory. But you're not going? Let me offer you a drink?'

But Calder, lean and eager, was straining at the leash – the sort of bloke who jogged half a dozen miles before breakfast, thought Rupert.

'Odd,' Oliver said, when Calder had been escorted to the hall by Miranda, 'I thought everyone at the BBC drank like fish. Speaking of which, Rupert, I wouldn't say no to a large whisky myself.'

'Oh not just yet, Oliver,' May said, as Miranda came back into the room. 'I have something to say to you first.'

'Fire away, my dear, fire away. If it's anything to do with money, you're unlikely to find me in a better mood to disburse.'

'No, it's nothing to do with money. At least,' said May, suddenly uncertain, 'I don't think so.'

'No,' Rupert said, coming to sit next to his daughter on the couch. 'It's nothing to do with money.'

'So you're in on this, are you? You too, Miranda?'

'Yes, I suppose I – yes, I am.'

'Right then, May my dear, spit it out – spit it out.'

'Dr Bowson wants me to go into hospital for a week or two.'

'Hospital? Why?'

'They want to regulate my pills – you know how muzzy they've been making me feel and how they've been upsetting my insides.'

'Yes. And can they cure that?' He reached out and straightened the pile of books on the table beside him.

'Well, they're simply side effects, you see, like my loss of taste and smell and. . . .' A movement by Miranda made her hesitate. 'Have I got that wrong, dear?'

'No no – I didn't mean – go on, Granny.'

'Well, you see – you see, with. . . .' May tightened her fist as if to stop the thread slipping from her grasp. 'With a little experimenting, they –'

'Experimenting? I'm not sure I like the sound of anyone experimenting on you, May.'

Miranda spoke firmly. 'It's not experimenting in that sense, Grandad. It's simply a question of substituting one pill for another until they hit on a combination which won't have the side effects.'

May sighed. 'Thank you, my dear.'

'Well, that sounds perfectly reasonable. What's all the fuss about?'

'No one's making a fuss, Oliver – unless you're going to.'

'Fuss? Why should I make a fuss? It all seems perfectly plain sailing.' He paused with a slight frown. 'The only point I'm not clear about is why such a thing should take two weeks – or why it should have to be done in hospital at all, for that matter.'

'Well,' May said reluctantly, 'there is something else.'

'Ah. I thought so. Not heart, is it?'

'Oh nothing like that. Dr Bowson says my heart is as strong as a horse and will last me till I'm a hundred – perish the thought! No, it's physiotherapy.'

'But you're not mad!'

'Not psychotherapy,' Rupert said gently, 'physiotherapy. For her knees, you know.'

'Oh. What's wrong with your knees? I mean, what do they want to do to them?'

'I gather they think they can make them better.' May's voice was tremulous with doubt. 'Isn't that it? Miranda, perhaps you could. . . .'

'What it really means,' Miranda said in a bright medical manner that caused Rupert to wince, 'is a short course of massage and manipulation – learning to exercise the muscles so that Granny will be a bit more mobile.'

'*Mobile*?' Oliver pronounced the word as though he had never before encountered it.

'Look, Grandad, if it goes according to plan, she should be able to – well, to potter about the garden again, even to get down to the end of the road.'

'What for?' said Oliver. 'There's nothing at the end of the road.'

May's hand unclenched in a mute motion of hopelessness.

'With any luck,' said Rupert quickly, 'it'll mean May will be able to get up and down the stairs much more easily and with far less strain – that's the really important thing.'

'And Oliver,' May said, brightening a little, 'we won't need the stairlift then, after all, and you won't have to worry about the cost and the inconvenience and –'

'Where your health and comfort are concerned, my dearest, cost is not a consideration – money is absolutely *no* object.' He took a pipe from the rack. 'The only thing that worries me is this physio- what's-it business – isn't that the thing you found such fearful agony when that frog-faced woman came and did it to you at the house?'

'Yes, dear – but Miranda says it will be different this time.'

'They're bound to give her an umbrella injection, which means,' Miranda said, hastily forestalling a question from Oliver, 'an injection that will kill pain in any of the affected areas during the process of manipulating the knees.'

'And what happens when the injection wears off?'

'Well,' said Miranda, slightly taken aback, 'why, then she'll have her ordinary pain-killing pills.'

'But I thought you just said they were going to take those away.'

'No, dear,' May said, 'not take them away –'

'Then I've got it all wrong.'

Rupert intervened. 'They're simply going to substitute the painkillers she has now for other painkillers that are different but equally effective.'

'I don't get it. Why?'

'Because they think the present painkillers in combination with her other pills may be causing the unpleasant side-effects.'

'Ah. Yes, I can grasp that.' He blew through the empty pipe. 'In that case I can see not the slightest cause for alarm.'

'No, Oliver, there isn't any,' said May. 'I just thought you might be a little worried that –'

'Worried? Why should I be worried? I'm sure they'll take infinitely better care of you in hospital than I can here.'

There was a soft collective murmur of relief. May smiled. 'It wasn't quite that – I thought you might be worried by my not being here.'

'Why should I be?'

'Yes, exactly,' Miranda said briskly. 'That's what I say. After all, you'll have Vi and – and Mrs Hamilton and Maud Pitchford and –'

'Can't stand Maud Pitchford.'

'And if you really get anxious,' Miranda swept on, 'you could always hire a car and go and see Granny in hospital yourself.'

'I can't afford a car. I don't like cars. I'd rather stay at home.'

'Look,' said Rupert, 'if there's a –'

But Miranda cut him off. 'You can phone her then – or if there isn't a phone by the bed, she can ring you from one of the telephone trolleys.'

'I'd rather not,' Oliver said. 'I detest the telephone.'

He returned the pipe to the rack.

'Oh dear, Oliver, you are being a bit difficult,' May said miserably. 'I really wonder whether I should go, after all.'

Oliver struggled forward on his chair. 'I'm not being in the least difficult. Of course you should go.' He stood up, steadying himself on the mantelpiece. 'You mustn't worry about me. I'm perfectly capable of looking after myself. And now, if you'll excuse me, I have one or two notes to make.'

Shoulders hunched, clutching at the furniture as he passed, he shuffled slowly out of the room.

'Oh dear oh dear.' May was close to tears.

'I'm sorry, Granny, I'm afraid I put my foot in it a bit.'

'No, dear, it's not your fault. He's always like that. What *am* I going to do?'

Rupert stood up and went over to the fire. 'I have – a suggestion,' he said slowly. It was perfectly obvious when one thought about it, yet he hesitated. In the front garden, Calder was talking and waving his arms and the designer was nodding. Then they turned and moved towards the gate.

'If it's all right with you, May, I'm game to stay on and keep Oliver company while you're in hospital.'

May looked up at him. 'Oh,' she said tremulously, 'oh, Rupert, would you?'

'I don't see why not – I've nothing much else to do just at the moment.'

'Oh Poopa, you angel!'

May blew her nose and shook her head doubtfully, 'It *would* be a load off my mind, but –'

'But he's a bit of a handful? Yes, I know. Perhaps I'd better go and see if he'll have me – before we start the celebration.'

'Alright, dear.' She managed a small smile. 'You know,' she said when Rupert had left the room, 'I shouldn't wonder if they didn't get on rather well together. Your grandfather is a difficult man, but then Rupert is very understanding – and so much more patient than I am.'

Miranda laughed. 'If patience is a virtue, Daddy must be the most virtuous man in England. I'm sure they'll get on like a house on fire.'

'I do hope not, dear. If there was ever a fire in this house, one would be burnt alive or overcome by smoke fumes long before one could unlock the doors or windows.'

After an anxiously rapid search, he found the old man at last sitting in the summerhouse reading the paper.

'Hello there!'

'What?' Oliver looked up wearily. 'Oh it's you. No, I shouldn't sit there if I were you, the wood's rotten – the other side's alright.'

Rupert sat down warily and lit a cigarette. 'Aren't you cold?' he said.

'Why should I be cold? The sun's shining – besides, it's always warm in here.'

'Look – Oliver . . . I'd be perfectly prepared to come and stay here with you while May's away in hospital.'

'You?'

'If you could put up with me.'

'Put up with you?' Oliver gave a crooked little smile. 'I think you'll find the boot would be on the other foot. I'm a frightful old curmudgeon, you know.'

'Well, the general opinion seems to be that I'm becoming rather an old bore.'

'What absolute nonsense. But, look here, Rupert, wouldn't it be the most frightful imposition?'

'For a fortnight? Not at all. I'd enjoy it. Besides I haven't – well, I haven't an awful lot to do just at the moment.'

'Oh?' Oliver lifted an eyebrow.

'The fact is,' he said in a sudden rush, 'I've left Sylvia – and given up schoolmastering.'

'Have you indeed? Ummm.'

'You don't sound very surprised. Did Milly tell you?'

'She did drop a veiled hint to that effect. But I'm too old to be easily surprised by anything, you know.'

'Oh.' Rupert smoked in silence, watching the birds busy at the bird table and hopping hopefully about on the ragged grass.

'I'm most frightfully grateful to you, you know,' said Oliver.

'What? Oh – yes. . . .' He looked closely at his father. 'What else did Milly say to you?'

'Well, as a matter of fact,' Oliver said with a light chuckle, 'she offered to bump me off – if I felt so inclined.'

'Bump you . . . good God! How? Why?'

'Oh nothing violent, you know – I'd hardly cast Miranda for the role of Lizzie Borden. Pills and whisky is the favoured mode of operation, so she informs me. She made it sound extremely easy.'

'Dammit, Oliver – I'm sorry. She must be out of her mind.' Rupert glanced angrily at the house – was she suggesting the same thing to May?

'No no, my boy, you mustn't take it amiss – I don't.'

'Well, I do.' Rupert felt his face flushing. 'It's damned impudence to come down here and –'

'I did ask her to come, you know.'

'I know you did,' but not, he thought, as the ministering angel of death. 'That's hardly an excuse.'

'Come come, Rupert. She was merely exhibiting the salutary ruthlessness of the young. I find it refreshing – it reminds me of myself. And she has a point – after all, we're not doing much more than cluttering up the landscape. There's a lot to be said for euthanasia.'

Rupert shook his head and dropped his cigarette on the boards and trod on it. 'Being young doesn't confer some kind of God-given right to be insensitive.'

'Perhaps not, but in some professions – mine, for instance, one has to have the hide of a rhinoceros. And a great deal of gall. I blush to think of some of the things I've done – the schemes I put over which I'd just thought up on the spur of the moment and hadn't the faintest idea how to carry out or even if they could be carried out at all. But I was lucky. I've always been lucky as a matter of fact. I was lucky in my marriage too – I'd have achieved very little without your mother – very little.'

Rupert lit another cigarette.

'I'd be lost without her, you know.'

'Yes.' Rupert roused himself. 'But you're not going to lose her just yet. This hospital thing – there's no operation involved or anything like that. She's probably in more danger here from falling down the stairs than she would be in hospital.'

'Do you think so? I hadn't thought of that. You're a great comfort. It's even an odd sort of comfort to know that one day you'll have this house.'

'I'd rather have you than the house.'

'Well, you haven't got it yet,' he said with a smile that took any sting from the words. 'And when you do, I hope it will be in rather better shape than it is now. If this BBC money comes through, I shall do the place up a bit, the paintwork at any rate – what do you think?'

'Calder likes it as it is.'

'Does he? The more I see of humanity, the barmier it seems to be. Although he has some very sound views on television, I must say.'

Rupert stood up. 'Do you feel like going in?'

'No, but don't let me stop you. I shall stay here a little longer – as long as the sun lasts.' He paused. 'You know, my boy, you have greatly relieved my mind, greatly. . . .'

'Good.' Rupert stepped down onto the grass. He turned. 'Oh by the way, why is the dustbin lid chained to the dustbin?'

'Against the foxes of course.'

'Oh yes.' Rupert smiled. 'Of course.'

Walking along the path at the side of the house, he glanced in at the sitting room window and halted. May and Miranda were talking with animation; there was something about the gestures or the angle of the head that betrayed their kinship – they were a pretty pair. Suddenly, as though aware of his stare, Miranda turned her head and, looking full at him, smiled.

Rupert nodded, but his anger, still on the boil, prevented him returning the smile. He was in no state to go in and make small talk.

'No, half a minute.' Miranda moved across the room closer to the back window. 'He's *not* coming in. He's stopped by the incinerator. He's doing something with the newspaper. Why, I do believe he's going to burn it.'

'He often does that – though it's usually only a page or two at a time.'

'Yes – he's lit it. There it goes! He's stepping back.' She turned to May. 'Why?'

'Now that I couldn't tell you. It's just one of his curious habits.'

'Perhaps he's burning the obituary page?'

'That's very clever of you – I hadn't thought of that one. But I don't believe there are obituaries on a Sunday, are there?' May looked up from her knitting as Miranda came back to the couch. 'Do you know, I've often wondered whether it mightn't have something to do with sex.'

'You mean – a sort of symbolic orgasm?'

'Do I? How interesting. I thought I was being rather fanciful. Surely old gentlemen of his age aren't interested in sex?'

'Oh yes, I think they might be. I'm sure of it in fact. There was a study done not so long ago, somewhere in America – we had it in geriatrics – about men and women in old-age homes where they segregate the sexes, in their seventies and eighties mostly. If they want to get married, they have to leave, and four out of five times when they did, the reason given wasn't for companionship or anything like that – but just for sex.'

'Well you do surprise me!' May lowered her knitting. 'I put a stop to that side of things over twenty years ago – after he had his first heart attack. I thought the strain might be bad for him. Do you think he's been frustrated all this time?'

'He could have been, I suppose.' Miranda grinned.

'It would account for a lot, wouldn't it? I must confess it was a great relief to me when it stopped.' She contemplated the fire for a few moments, then raised her head to Miranda. 'Tell me, my dear, if it isn't a rude question, are you much interested in sex?'

Caught off balance, Miranda blushed. 'Well, I think I have the – the normal instincts of a healthy woman,' she said, with a stilted little laugh.

'How very nice for you.' May sighed. 'I never could get on with it myself. Of course, sex was unmentionable in my home, so I was completely ignorant. I remember when I got my first period, my mother told me it was God's curse upon Eve. So very silly – why should God want to curse Eve? Or anyone else for that matter?'

'Wasn't it because she led Adam astray in the Garden of Eden? The original scapegoating procedure.'

'I've always found that part of the Old Testament quite incomprehensible.' She picked up her knitting, then put it down again. 'I'll tell you what *I* think God's curse upon women is,' she said with sudden vehemence. 'Old age and infirmity. When you've been active and practical and good at things, if you know what I mean, it's exceedingly trying to be stuck in one place and to see inferior meals being served up and your house getting shabbier and shabbier without being able to do anything about it.

Sometimes I feel as though I'm glassed in like some exhibit in a museum – which no one can possibly want to see and never being able to get out. I might just as well be imprisoned in that Pyramid of his.'

'Granny – would you like me to wheel you out in the Park a bit this afternoon?'

'Yes, dear, that would be very nice. But I was speaking generally, you know.'

'Yes, I realize that.' She hesitated. 'Granny, I know that it's worse now – now that you can't get about at all – but wasn't marriage always confining . . . for a woman of your generation?'

'Oh dear me no – quite the reverse. Marriage was a release for women like me. I always had to earn my own living, you see, and in those days the field was rather restricted. First I was a governess in Germany for a year – that was a dreadful time, the Germans are so strict and sloppy about their children. After that I was a schoolmistress, which I enjoyed up to a point, but, delightful as young girls can be, they do rather limit one's mental horizons. Then during the War I was an officer in the WAACs – that was a real eye-opener to me – one had had absolutely *no* idea of the way working-class women behaved. I suppose I had led a rather sheltered life up to then, but *that* made me realize how much there was to be done.' She looked down at the knitting on her lap and sighed.

'What did you do after the war?'

'After the War? Well, I had rather an unfortunate experience.' She paused. 'A love affair – what *we* called a love affair, it didn't involve sex in those days.'

'What – happened?'

'Nothing, my dear. He was a very nice young man – intelligent and gay and amusing – and I was very fond of him. He was very pressing for me to marry him. But he'd lost both his legs on the Western Front, poor lad, just above the knee. And I really honestly felt I couldn't take on a cripple for the rest of my life.' She looked at Miranda. 'Does that shock you?'

'I – I'm not sure,' she said doubtfully. She went over to the fire and poked it absent-mindedly. 'No I don't think so – I expect it was the sensible thing to do, but. . . .' She put the poker back on its stand and straightened up. 'What happened to him, your soldier?'

'He went to live up North, with a married sister, I believe. We still exchange Christmas cards – though come to think of it, I don't recollect receiving one last year.'

'And he didn't marry?'

'Not so far as I know. Now why don't you get yourself a drink, my dear? I expect you need it after all this family history – and it's no use waiting for Rupert, he seems to have taken himself off somewhere.'

'To the pub, I expect.' She poured herself some of the malt and added a little water. From where she stood she could see the old man – he'd finished his ritual burning and was making his way slowly towards the house, the remains of the paper folded neatly under his arm.

'And where did you meet Grandad?'

'We always say we met in a fish shop – which is more or less true.' She picked up her knitting. It was time to start turning the heel, which was going to demand all her attention. 'You see, when Rupert went away, I –'

'Rupert?'

'"My soldier", as you call him. I was always fond of the name. Well, when he left, I had to turn and make my living again. I got a job doing publicity for a new chain of fish shops that was just opening. I had to go along in advance to the towns where each new shop was to be opened and make sure that everything was done with the proper fanfare – hire a band, butter up the local Chamber of Commerce, collar the mayor to make a speech if possible, put advertisements in the local press, all that sort of thing. It was at one of those openings that I met Oliver – he was involved in the design of the shops, and he gave a little talk about it. I went up to him afterwards and said, "I bet you've never bought a piece of fish in your life." "No," he said, "I haven't." "And what's more," I said, "I bet you couldn't tell me the difference between mackerel and hake if your life depended on it." "No," he said, "I couldn't – why don't you tell me?" So I did. A week later he proposed. And we've never looked back. But surely I must have told you that story a thousand times before?'

'No – never.'

May looked up at her and they smiled at one another.

'Well – now we ought to be thinking about the lunch.'

'Yes of course.' Miranda took a large swig of whisky. 'What should I do first?'

'Heat the oven and peel the potatoes and put them in with plenty of fat in the pan. And then – do you know how to prepare Brussels sprouts?'

'Oh yes,' said Miranda, 'of course I do.'

'Ugly, isn't it?' said a voice behind him.

Rupert turned with a start to the clergyman who had padded up so silently. 'Well . . . it doesn't have a great deal to recommend it.' It was a Victorian edifice of seamless banality, with not a single redeeming idiosyncracy. 'But. . . .'

'But what matters is what is put into the vessel?' He laughed. 'I am the vicar by the way – Martin Jones. You are a newcomer to the parish?'

'No – not really.' He didn't want to talk to this smiling young man who looked about seventeen – he'd only wandered into the church because there was ten minutes to spare before the pub across the road opened. 'I used to live here – but I'm afraid I've only ever been in this church once in my life.'

'*Not* a Christian then?' the vicar enquired amiably.

'Not exactly – rather off and on.'

'You mustn't let that discourage you.'

Rupert frowned – there was nothing encouraging about this church without a soul and this boy without a beard.

'And what was the occasion of your previous attendance?' The vicar put a hand on Rupert's arm. 'A wedding? A christening?'

'A christening, actually,' Rupert said, repressing the impulse to shake off the clergyman's paw.

'A member of the family, no doubt?' he said, gently nudging Rupert down the aisle.

'My daughter,' Rupert said shortly, increasing his pace.

'A daughter – terrific!'

Rupert stopped abruptly and stared at the vicar, then he laughed.

Mr Jones dropped his hand and looked at Rupert with a bewildered smile.

'I'm sorry – it's just that . . . I'm sorry. I expect you want to lock up, don't you?' He stepped into the porch.

'Yes, I'm afraid we do have to lock up, deplorable as it is, particularly on a Sunday. But we suffer from petty pilferers and vandals, I'm sorry to say, even in this neighbourhood.' Having almost pushed Rupert out of the church, he now seemed anxious to detain him. 'And I regret to say the people from the pub – well, when I tell you that three or four times we've had unfortunates coming in here and being sick in the pews, and once on the chancel steps. . . .'

'Safety first.' Rupert moved into the street. 'I'm sure you're absolutely justified. Goodbye.'

'Do you – do you? I'm so glad. Er – what was the name?'

'Miranda Judith. Goodbye!' he called, crossing the street. As he entered the pub, he saw the vicar still standing puzzled at the church gate.

He ordered a pint and ate little pieces of cheese from bowls on the counter. He was almost the first customer, and the pub had the expectant hush appropriate to a church. He'd treated the vicar rudely, but that christening twenty-five years ago was still a curious embarrassment. Quite what had made him insist on the christening over Sylvia's vehement protests he could no longer remember – some sense of the innate fitness of things, or perhaps just to be on the safe side (and nothing could be safer than the Church of England, infallible repository of compromise). The elderly vicar of the time had evidently found it hard to make contact with the laconic young couple that confronted him. Perhaps in any case he'd been a man happier with small talk.

'Good, good,' he'd said, winding up their one and only interview. 'Might I ask the significance of the Christian names you have chosen?'

'*The Tempest*,' said Rupert.

'Judith of Bethulia,' said Sylvia.

'How interesting. Interesting. Personally I always find it a little difficult to come to terms with the moral implications of Judith's actions – don't you?'

'Why?' said Sylvia. 'She didn't fornicate with Holofernes, you know – she only cut off his head.'

'Quite, quite.' But as they left, the vicar had taken Rupert aside for a moment. 'Are you sure that you and your wife are, er, fully conversant with the nature of the sacrament?'

'Oh absolutely,' Rupert had said airily. But he had not realized (having been rebaptized in the Church of Rome as an adult) that the whole gamut of sin and wickedness could be imputed to an infant of two months. Exhorted to get rid of the Old Adam in her, Miranda had quite justifiably shrieked throughout the entire proceedings.

'Well,' May had said afterwards as they came out of church, 'at least we can be sure that the devil got out.'

'If the devil is responsible for the carnal desires of the flesh, I'd like to find some ceremony for putting him back in again,' Sylvia had replied.

'Would you, my dear?' May had said sweetly. 'But there is such a ceremony – it's called marriage.'

Rupert laughed out loud.

'The same again, sir?'

'Yes – no. Make it a large whisky.'

> Who's been polishing the sun,
> Sweeping all the clouds away?
> They must have known just how I like it,
> Everything's coming my –

'Hello, somebody's been mucking about with the fire,' said

Oliver, returning to the hearth with a replenished glass.

'Yes, dear. We can't all sit here freezing to death while you're gallivanting about the garden, you know.'

'Well well, no harm done.' He gave the coals a prod with the toe of his shoe, then turned his back to the fire. 'Although it's remarkably mild out this morning – not as warm as yesterday of course, but it makes one feel that winter has shot its bolt.' He swirled the liquid in the glass and hummed to himself.

'Miranda is going to take me for a little turn in the Park this afternoon.'

'Is she, by Jove?' He drank. 'On the whole we've been rather lucky with our progeny.'

'Luck has nothing to do with it. If it had been up to you, we wouldn't have any progeny. I hope you've thanked Rupert properly.'

'Of course I have. It's a noble offer. Though no great sacrifice for him in the circumstances – which is why I made no bones about accepting at once.'

May looked up sharply. 'What do you mean by "circumstances"?'

'Why, that he's left Sylvia – surely he's told you?'

'Oh yes – he told *me*.'

'I see – it was I who was supposed to be kept in the dark, was it?' He smiled. 'Well, my dear, I'm hardly likely to be knocked sideways by *that* piece of news – I've seen it coming for years.'

'That's exceedingly clever of you,' May said dryly, 'it's more than Rupert did.'

'Doubtless. But then for all his many excellent qualities, Rupert is inclined to be a wee bit slow on the uptake at times. I should have left that woman after six months.'

'If she hadn't left you after three.'

'Which would have been highly probable.' He straightened his waistcoat. 'It takes a lot of gumption to stick to me.'

'Really, Oliver, you are incorrigible,' May said with an exasperated smile.

'Am I, my darling? And I'm feeling at my most reasonable.' He sat down, carefully keeping the glass level. 'You know, I was very interested in what that BBC chap was saying.'

'Yes – wasn't it a coincidence?'

'Wasn't what a coincidence?'

'Archdeacon Calder being his great-uncle.'

'Oh that! I don't give a fig for his family connections – he could be second cousin to the king of the Zulus for all I care. I was thinking of what he said about television.'

'Exceedingly sniffy, I thought. We used to call that biting the hand that feeds you.'

'No no, my dear, he wasn't against television *per se* – he was against *bad* television.'

'And we're all against sin.'

'Ah, but that analogy won't hold water.' He took a judicious swallow of his drink. 'Sin adds a bit of spice to things – if it wasn't exciting, it wouldn't be sin. And this chap's point was that television was mostly as dull as ditchwater, not that it was too exciting.'

'What about violence and the teenagers?'

'What *about* violence and the teenagers?' Oliver said testily. 'I can tell you something quite categorically – I'd far rather have teenagers subject to violence on the screen than on the battlefield.'

May opened her mouth to make a snappish reply, but then shook her head. 'Yes, dear. I'm sorry I spoke.'

'Well – what was my point? Ah yes – my point is that this fellow Calder said there were several excellent programmes from time to time. And he impressed me as a man of sound judgment. So – if this BBC money comes through – I've decided to buy us a television set.'

May put down her knitting and gave Oliver a long, enquiring look. 'That's very kind of you, but I don't think you quite know what you'd be letting yourself in for.'

'Oh yes I do. I've thought it all out. You're afraid I'll be bored – but I have no intention of being bored. If I am, I shall go and read in my studio or take myself off to bed. Now don't try to talk me out of it; I have quite made up my mind.'

After a moment of silence, May nodded to herself and uttered a small sigh. 'Thank you, Oliver.'

'Don't thank me – thank your archdeacon's grand nephew.' He waved a hand expansively. 'It's the only sensible thing to do. I've been a dog in the manger about all this far too long. The only thing that matters, my darling, is your happiness.'

May bowed and permitted herself a smile.

'Besides,' said Oliver, taking a hefty draught of whisky, 'I'm bound to enjoy some of the programmes myself.'

Rupert walked in at the open back door to find Miranda crouched at the oven.

'God, there you are at last! How did Granny say he liked his potatoes – underdone or overdone?'

'Overdone.'

'Then they need more time.' She slammed the oven door and stood up. 'Where have you been? Slurping it up at the boozer, while I've been slaving over a hot stove.' Her cheeks were flushed, but her semi-belligerent air was spoiled by an absurdly frilly plastic apron – undoubtedly one of Vi's.

Rupert laughed.

'It's all very well for you to laugh, but, look, I've burnt my finger on that wretched old oven.'

'Put some butter on it,' Rupert said, with a cursory glance.

'Butter!' She went over to the sink. 'You must have learned your first aid in the middle ages.' As she turned on the tap, the rubber nozzle fell off and shot a spray of cold water in her face.

Subduing a grin, Rupert perched himself on the table and lit a cigarette. 'I had a nice little chat with the vicar.'

'Shit!' said Miranda, mopping her face with a dish towel. 'Nothing works in this grungy old house.'

'Could do with a bit of a face-lift. As a matter of fact, Oliver says he's going to spend some money on it – if your Roy Calder lives up to his promises.'

'What do you mean, *my* Roy Calder?'

'I thought he was in a fair way to being rather a friend of yours.'

'God, Daddy – you've got sex on the brain.'

Rupert laughed again, and Miranda gave him a hard stare. 'Are you drunk?'

'I don't think so.' Two pints and a couple of large whiskies – hardly.

Miranda shrugged and hung up the towel. 'I suppose I don't blame you. Living in this place would drive anyone to drink.'

'I'm not going to *live* here – I'm just going to stay until May's safely back from hospital.'

'That's what you say now, but I know you,' she said with a sigh, 'you'll never get away.'

'I certainly shall,' he said indignantly. 'I've got my own life to lead. Of course, if they needed me, I'd be prepared to stay on a bit, but –'

'Pooh! That's got nothing to do with it. Look how you hung on at Brighton long after Mum had any use for you.'

'That – that's a bit harsh.'

'Maybe it is, but it's the truth. You're just rationalizing the course of least resistance with a lot of high-minded blather! When –'

'That damned psychiatric textbook!'

'– when I was a little kid and needed you desperately, you were off doing your thing in Paris or Peru. You didn't care a damn. For all I knew, you could have been dead!'

'I'm sorry, Milly,' he said slowly, 'I didn't know.' He was stone-cold sober now. 'Perhaps these days I'm a little – wiser. And if the old folk need me . . . I shall be here.'

'What they need is a quick clean death! The best thing that could happen to them would be to die together in a fatal car crash.'

'What an absolutely foul thing to say!' Anger flooded him. 'I suppose that's why you offered to help Oliver commit suicide.'

'Oh, he told you, did he?'

'Yes, he did. Good God, Milly – just how brutal can you get?'

'It's not brutal,' she shouted at him, 'it's practical!'

'Practical? So I suppose you suggested the same thing to May?'

He squashed his cigarette on a saucer with a trembling hand.

'Get off, Daddy – you don't understand anything.'

'No, I don't! I don't understand how you've got the gall to come here with your beastly little eugenic ideas and –'

'Oh shit!' She pulled the apron over her head and threw it at him.

'Milly!'

'You finish the bloody lunch,' she said and marched past him and out of the back door.

'Damn.' As the angry pulse of blood in his ears ebbed and died, he stood up, aghast. The smell of over-cooked sprouts filled the kitchen. He looked down at the frilly plastic in his hands and clutched it tightly to him as if to stop the bottom dropping out of the world.

Rupert cautiously stirred the fire into a small blaze.

The old man snored softly, the after-lunch glass of whisky half empty at his side. The book spread out on his stomach moved in gentle time with his breathing. Rupert read the title upside down – *Plain or Ringlets*.

The longcase clock gave a grating whirr – it was two minutes before the hour. Outside, the afternoon was patchily brilliant, and the fitful sun was just at an angle to catch Vi's daffodils on the window table and make them glow.

Rupert went back to the couch and picked up the Sunday paper. The review section was unaccountably missing, so he turned to the business news: Industrialist says British Management is Incompetent and Effete.

Rupert yawned.

The clock struck four, its cocky little strike causing the old man to stir in his sleep.

'Pyramid,' he muttered, 'pyramid. . . .'

'Hold on, Granny – bump coming!' Miranda gingerly manoeuvred the wheelchair over a protruding root in the path. 'Alright?'

'Quite alright – very well managed.'

It was downhill for the moment and Miranda had little more to do than guide the chair. 'But what I meant was, Granny – all that was voluntary work, wasn't it?'

'Indeed it was. When I founded the Health Centre, it was quite a novel undertaking – at least for that part of London – but we had to raise every penny for it privately and we had to rely a good deal on people donating their services. Later on of course we began to get grants from the Council. My dear, do look at that squirrel – isn't he a joke?'

Miranda slowed the wheelchair as the squirrel cavorted on a great broken branch on the ground. It ran briskly from one end to the other and back again, stopped in the middle, did a loop the loop, then stood on its hind legs chattering at them.

'I do believe he's giving a performance just for us,' May said as the squirrel started the routine again. 'You know, when we first came to live here it was almost exclusively red squirrels, then gradually the grey squirrels began to appear and over the years they drove the red variety away until there wasn't a single one left.'

They walked on in silence for a while – even going uphill was very little effort, for May seemed to weigh practically nothing.

'But what sort of people came to the Centre? I mean, what was the basis of selection?'

'Need, my dear. Of course our service was for mothers or women with babies on the way, but as far as I recollect we never said no to any of them. Most of them were very poor and a lot of them unmarried – they had very little notion of hygiene and their ideas about cooking were limited to opening tins of baked beans or salmon. Now, you see that house up there on the left?' May pointed a gloved hand. 'That's White Lodge, where the Queen used to live when she was a little girl, with Princess Margaret – or Margaret Rose as she was called then. They were very pretty little girls, though of course one didn't see much of them – except in the back of a Daimler.'

'Shall we go on – or have you had enough?'

'I'm quite prepared to go on, if you are?'

'Oh yes. I just thought you might be getting cold.'

'No, I'm quite warm and cosy, thank you – and I can *feel* the fresh air doing me good.'

'Right you are.' After a few yards, they came clear of the trees and in view of the Pen Ponds with the sun glittering on the surface of the water. May gave a little murmur of approval, but Miranda was more concerned with picking a smooth path.

'All the same, Granny,' she said, 'you're only talking about one fairly small area – but there must have been heaps of people who didn't get any help. And now everyone does – or has the right to.'

'That's quite true. Why, all I have to do is pick up the phone and in the twinkling of an eye I'd have a social worker round and the district nurse and a woman to come and give me baths twice a week. But it's a job – something they're paid to do. I'm not decrying it, but it's not like the old days when we did it because we wanted to do it – one saw a need and one turned to and did one's best to answer it. Oh – aren't the deer enchanting? Do stop for a moment.'

Obediently Miranda halted. The sun still shone, but there was a chill in the air and a hint of rain.

'What you're really talking about is the quality of care, aren't you, Granny? But in a caring society –'

'I've never understood that phrase, I'm afraid. How can a *society* care? The society can spend money, but surely it's only *people* who can care?'

'Alright – but being paid doesn't mean one doesn't care.'

'Far be it from me to suggest such a thing. Still, one can't purchase compassion, can one? But of course you know all about that – otherwise why would you have chosen to be a doctor?' May turned her head so that Miranda could see the faint smile on her lips. 'Now, dear, you'll have to be a little careful on the next patch – if I remember rightly, it's inclined to be rather boggy.'

Oliver opened his eyes quite suddenly and fully. His hands slowly tightened on the arms of the chair until the knuckles were white.

He panted softly. His left hand moved and began to creep upward towards his waistcoat pocket. He hiccoughed.

Rupert woke up. 'Oliver – are you. . . .' He slid off the couch and knelt at the old man's side.

'Pill,' Oliver whispered, 'pocket. . . .'

Rupert had the pill box in his hand in a moment; he took out a white pill and carefully placed it under Oliver's tongue. 'Water?'

Oliver shook his head faintly, shut his eyes. Very slowly he opened his hand and Rupert reached down and clasped it. They remained hand in hand as the clock ticked away the minutes. The fire shifted slightly.

Oliver shuddered and opened his eyes.

'Better?' said Rupert.

'I shall . . . be alright,' he answered breathlessly, 'in a minute. . . .'

'Don't try to talk.'

The old man muttered something.

'What?'

'I said . . . like talking . . . nothing else to do.' He tightened his grip, then gradually loosened it. 'This stuff – works fast.' He turned his eyes to Rupert. 'Don't worry – happens quite often.'

'Shouldn't I give Bowson a ring?'

Oliver frowned. 'No earthly use ringing him – can't help. Never there – on Sundays – anyway.' He released Rupert's hand and took the yellow handkerchief from his breast pocket and wiped his mouth. 'Working now . . . much better already.'

'Anything I can get you?'

'Nothing. Sorry about this.' He smiled apologetically. 'Come and sit down here by me. Something I want to tell you.'

'Hadn't you better take it easy?' Rupert said, pulling the poufe over and sitting down.

'I am taking it easy,' he said, his voice a little stronger. 'Now. My will. Everything goes to you – although May has the use of the house during her lifetime of course – but I want Miranda to have the Pyramid. By that I mean she should take charge of the plans, the various drafts, my notes and diary – the whole kit and caboodle. I've made no formal provision as yet, but Miranda understands all about it – I've had a long talk with her. That's why I asked her down. You understand?'

'Yes, Oliver, I understand.'

'Good. I thought it best, you see, to skip a generation. But you are my executor – and I want you to keep an eye on her. If there are any problems, it's up to you to do what you think best.'

'Yes, of course. But I don't think there should be any problems.'

'You never know. She might marry a rotter. Women are strange creatures.'

Rupert smiled. 'I think Milly's got her head screwed on all right.'

'Maybe, maybe.' He closed his eyes with a sudden air of strain – then gave a loud belch. 'That's better.' He sighed and opened his eyes. 'Now. My memorial service – you won't forget, will you? St Paul's, Covent Garden – the Club will give you a hand. And the Mozart violin concerto – the Turkish – the slow movement.' He made an effort to whistle the melody between his teeth, but hadn't the breath.

'I know the one you mean. I shan't forget.'

'I'm sure you won't, my boy. I shall go upstairs in a minute.'

'Hadn't you better stay here for a bit?'

'No. Always go upstairs. Don't want your mother to see me like this. Only upsets her.' His eyelids fluttered, but he forced them open again. 'I have no regrets, you know. Though I should have liked a knighthood – a bauble, I know; the definitive mark of mediocrity – any second-rate actor or bankrupt businessman gets a knighthood these days. All the same.' He chuckled. 'But I was too independent. Spoke my mind and offended all the toadies.'

'Are you sure I shouldn't just give old Bowson a ring?'

'No. I mean, I am sure. I shall be all right.' He pushed himself onto the edge of the chair. 'Give me a hand up.'

Rupert caught hold of his hands and gently pulled him to his feet.

'That's better. Just let me get my breath.'

'Here, take my arm.'

'No thanks.' He began to move slowly, dragging his feet across the carpet. 'I can manage perfectly well by myself.' He fumbled with the door handle, got the door open, then turned with his lop-sided little smile. 'Don't you worry about me, my boy.'

Rupert went straight into the studio. The north light fell full and clear on the expanse of the plan on the wall. Rupert studied it, now and again moving close to examine a detail – he whistled when he saw the scale – then stepping back to view the whole. He smiled and scratched the back of his neck. 'Pyramid,' he murmured and shook his head.

At the beginning Oliver had sometimes talked about his Pyramid – he had still been active enough to get round to the pub with Rupert and sit in the garden there drinking stout and smoking his pipe and letting his imagination go – but as time passed he had said less and less until in later years he had not mentioned it at all. But Rupert remembered enough of the beginning (which had sometimes seemed no more than a flight of fancy) to grasp something of the achievement of the end – the mad splendour of vision made real in every detail and set on earth, or on paper.

He returned to the sitting room and looked vaguely round – perhaps he could get Oliver to explain eventually. Or Milly – 'Miranda understands all about it – I've had a long talk. . . .' It was not talk that Rupert wanted. The house was always full of words, where once it had been filled with music.

He flipped quickly through the records, then, lifting the vase of flowers to the floor, he opened the lid of the radiogram and put on an old seventy-eight. It was scratchy with age, but above the hiss, the sound of the violin swum clear and clean as the flight of a seagull.

Rupert stood still, listening – then, spreading his arms, he slowly began to dance.

'The children really look so very bright and gay in their coloured wellingtons,' May said on their way back. 'I remember how drab and uniform children's clothes tended to be in the old days. I quite thought that little boy in the scarlet jacket was going to fall in – he was so very intrepid. He rather reminded me of your father when he was small – he was exceedingly fond of the water, in any shape or form, I may say.'

'Daddy? Was he?' Miranda slowed down as a spaniel came racing towards them with menacing barks, then turned playfully aside at the last moment. 'Maybe that's why we moved to Brighton – to be by the sea. Mum hates it.'

'I recollect he had one very curious little rite he used to perform when it was very cold. He used to fill one of my larger vases and put it out overnight, so in the morning it was frozen solid. Then he would turn it out onto a pan in front of the sitting room fire – so that he had a sort of large ice bullet. He'd heat the poker till it was red hot, then plunge it into the ice. It made a very satisfactory hissing noise.'

Miranda laughed, 'How weird!'

'Do you think so? Perhaps it was. Of course he was eight or nine at the time. He carved it with the utmost care, you know – and really made some quite beautiful, well, sculptures I suppose they were.'

'But they must have melted pretty quickly.'

'Yes, and how very cross he used to get about it. Oh dear, look at that silly little lady tantalizing her dog with the stick. Throw it, my good woman, throw it!'

'It looks like Mrs Hamilton to me.'

'Does it? Dear me, then I'd better mind my p's and q's.'

Rupert halted suddenly, poised for a moment, then turned off the record.

He raised his head – a flake of plaster fell from the ceiling as the thumping came again.

He ran out of the room and took the stairs two at a time.

'Doesn't Vi ever take you out?' Miranda said, turning out of the Park gates into the road.

'Not if I can help it – she bumps me about most dreadfully. She's like one of those maddening drivers who are always pointing things out to you on one side of the road or another, instead of looking where they're going. It quite puts my heart in my mouth.'

A solitary horsewoman with a timeless leathern face gave them a brief nod as she clopped by.

'That's Barbara Maitland – she's been running the local stables for, oh, going on for thirty years, I suppose, by now. They say she drinks, but I don't believe it – she doesn't look a day older than when she started. Not like poor Hazel Maybury who shows more and more of the effects of gin with every passing month. And she makes such a to-do about accepting a small glass of sherry. Really rather a tiresome woman. Now, *that* house, the angular shaped one – has a sad little story connected with it. . . .'

'Yes. Right – you'll get on to them directly then. How long are they likely to be? . . . I see. Alright. And meanwhile there's nothing I can do. . . . Keep him warm, yes, I've got that. Goodbye.' He put down the phone.

Oliver lay askew on the bed with his legs dangling over the side. His eyes were open, staring unflickering at the ceiling. One hand clutched the Rhodes sponge close to his chest, in the other he held the unopened pill box.

Rupert lifted the legs onto the bed and put a pillow under Oliver's head. He tried tentatively to remove the sponge, but Oliver's fingers tightened and he made a faint moan.

'Don't worry – the ambulance will be along soon.' He took the eiderdown from May's bed and spread it over the old man.

Taking the box of matches from the mantelpiece, he knelt down and lit the gas fire and turned it up full. He glanced at his watch. It would take half an hour to take the chill off the room, and by that time. . . .

He heard the sound of voices and the click of the gate and got to the window in time to see Milly wheeling May towards the back door. But they didn't notice him when he waved.

'That was the best outing I've had in many a long day,' May said as Miranda helped her off with her coat. 'I'm most appreciative.'

'Well, we'll do it again soon.'

'I hope so, my dear, I hope so.' She took Miranda's arm and hobbled into the sitting room. 'You really are a first-class wheeler – hello, everyone's flown the coop.'

'Shall I go and see where they've got to?'

'I shouldn't bother – I expect they're sleeping it off upstairs. But I wouldn't say no to a drop of tea.'

'That's a good idea, Granny. I'll go and put the kettle on.'

May eased herself into the chair and spread the shawl over her knees. She switched on the light and, noticing the open radiogram and the vase of flowers on the floor, gave a little smile and a nod.

'Milly!' Rupert said in a loud whisper, leaning over the banisters.

'Hello, Daddy – what are you doing up there?'

'Come on up – quietly – the old man's had an attack.'

Still in her red raincoat, she ran swiftly up the stairs. 'What sort of an attack?'

'I don't know – serious, I'm afraid.' He followed her into the bedroom.

'Why the sponge?' said Miranda, turning back the eiderdown and taking the old man's wrist.

'I don't know – he must have grabbed it at some point. What do you think?'

Miranda shook her head silently. She took her fingers from his wrist and covered him again.

'His colour's bad – and I can hardly get his pulse.'

'Then it *is* something more than an angina attack?'

'Yes.'

'A stroke?'

'A coronary, I think. Have you called an ambulance?'

'Yes. Or rather, I rang Bowson's surgery and got the weekend doctor who said he'd do it right away.'

'Okay. Did he say how long?'

'About ten minutes normally – but with the strike, well, they may have to use St John's Ambulance. Still, that shouldn't make too much difference – St Mary's is only on the other side of the Park.'

They turned to the window. 'On a clear day you can see the hospital clock tower from here.' But it had completely clouded over – and there was a fine mist of rain not far away.

Miranda said, 'They'd better get a move on.'

'Yes. Well. I must go and tell May. You stay here.'

'Yes.'

'And Milly – I'll let the ambulance men in, but would you go along with him to the hospital?'

'Whatever you say.'

'I ought to stay with May – but Oliver shouldn't be left alone.'

Miranda nodded. 'Alright, Daddy. That makes sense.' She turned back to the bed.

Oliver's eyes were closed now and his cheeks were a deep purplish blue. Except for the occasional stertorous breath, his respiration was barely detectable.

'Come on, Grandad,' she whispered softly.

'Hello, Rupert. Have you been having a little snooze?'

'May. . . .' He sat down on the couch and leaned forward.

She looked at him over the top of her glasses. 'Is it Oliver?'

Rupert nodded. 'He's had an attack.'

'Oh blow! It would happen when I wasn't there.'

'May, I'm afraid this is a bit more serious than the usual angina.'

'I see.' She paused. 'Is he dead?'

'No – but he's in quite a bad way. Milly thinks he's had a coronary. Bowson's locum's rung Emergency and an ambulance should be here any minute to take him to hospital.'

'Is Miranda up there with him now?'

'Yes.'

May took off her glasses and pinched the bridge of her nose

with her fingers. 'Hospital – the poor old lad. And it was I who was supposed to be going to hospital.'

'It won't be long now. Would you like a cup of tea?'

'Not just yet. A little later, perhaps.'

May cocked her head and raised her hand – and they heard the distant ululation of an ambulance.

Rupert stood. 'I must go and open up.'

'Are you – are you going with him?'

'No, my dear, I shan't leave you. I'll stay.' He moved to the door. 'Milly will go along – she'll be much more use than I would anyway.'

'Rupert.' May craned her neck round. 'Rupert – shall I see him?'

He paused with the door half open. 'I think better not – not now.'

The shrill *pam-pam* of the ambulance grew suddenly louder, reached a crescendo – stopped.

'Not now,' May repeated to the silence.

'Steady on!' Miranda called sharply, as the stretcher bumped against the handrail.

'Don't you worry, miss – we'll get him there in one piece,' said the ambulance man who'd staggered.

'Just get him down the stairs first.'

Strapped to the stretcher, Oliver was evidently a heavy load, but they were doing their best, thought Rupert as he held the front door open.

'Right,' said the ambulance man as they negotiated the final step and he gave Rupert a quick wink – or maybe he was just blinking away the sweat.

Oliver's eyes were shut and he seemed to be quite unconscious as they carried him out, though he still clutched the sponge.

'Blast them,' Miranda whispered fiercely to Rupert, 'they haven't got any oxygen equipment.'

'Is that important?'

'It might be vital.' Then she shrugged. 'I don't know. It's not their fault, I suppose – St John's ambulances are not automatically equipped apparently.'

'Ring me when you know what's what, Milly.'

'Yes, okay – either that, or I'll be back myself.'

He watched her run after the stretcher-bearers. He found the switch by the front door that lit the lamp over the garden gate and turned it on in time to see her climb into the ambulance. It was twilight already – in a few minutes it would be dark.

He shut the front door just as the siren started to shrill.

'No, no more tea, thank you.' May peered at the clock. 'To tell you the truth, I think I could do with a small whisky and water, if it wouldn't be too much trouble. It's very nearly six o'clock.'

Rupert stood up slowly and threw his cigarette into the fire. 'No trouble. Malt – or the ordinary kind?'

'The ordinary kind if you don't mind.' May had the sewing box onto her lap and was methodically re-arranging the contents. 'I never could abide just sitting and waiting. It makes one feel so helpless.'

Rupert nodded as he poured her whisky and then, after a moment's hesitation, a larger one for himself.

'My parents would have been down on their knees at this moment of course.'

'Well, we could do worse.' He gave her the glass.

'But it wouldn't make him come back if he's gone, would it? Thank you, my dear.'

'No, but. . . .' He shook his head and, pushing the tea trolley aside, sat down.

'And I don't think he is going to come back – not this time.'

'I wouldn't be sure,' he murmured half to himself, then, making an effort, 'The ambulance men seemed like very competent types.'

May gave him a quizzical look. 'Perhaps we should have offered them the best sherry.'

'Perhaps we should.' He laughed and swallowed some whisky. 'May. . . .'

'Yes, dear?'

'What ever happened to Lord?'

'Our old gardener?'

'Yes, the one who was stung in the throat by a bee.'

'Fancy you remembering that – I should have thought you'd have been far too young. He died.'

'Not from the bee sting?'

'Oh yes, he was allergic to them, you know.'

'Good Lord . . . stung to death by savage bees.'

'There was only one, and as far as I know it was the common or garden variety.' She compared two spools of thread under the light.

The clock struck six. Rupert looked at his watch – six it was. Only two hours ago, when it had struck four, he'd been sitting in the same place watching Oliver dozing comfortably in his chair . . . and two days ago, here too, talking of this and that, waiting for Milly . . . two years, twenty years. . . .

'Did I tell you Tudor Lodge sold for over two hundred thousand pounds the other day?'

'Was that the – what are they called – the Robinsons?'

'Yes. It's slightly smaller than this house, though of course the Robinsons had modernized it and put in central heating, she being American – which is bound to make a bit of difference.'

'Warmer.'

'I don't think it's anything to joke about. Surely you're hardly in the position at the moment to ignore the practical side of things.'

'What? Oh – oh no, perhaps not. . . .' He yawned, then stood up and stretched. He wandered vaguely about the room – straightened the pile of books on Oliver's table, shut the radiogram and replaced Mrs Hamilton's funereal flowers on top of it. They must have got to St Mary's at least half an hour ago.

'Rupert, as you're up, you might try and open a window – the key's in the left-hand pigeon-hole of my bureau.'

'Good idea.' He unscrewed the lock, but push and pull as he

would, the window remained stuck fast. 'I think it's been painted shut – when was it last opened?'

'I tremble to think. This room's been hermetically sealed for donkey's years.'

'I might see what I could do with a chisel.'

'No, don't bother now – it's just that I could have done with a breath of fresh air. I did have such a splendid outing with Miranda. Do you know, we went all the way to the Pen Ponds?'

'Did you indeed?' The garden was in darkness but a fine envelope of rain glittered in the light over the gate.

'One of the things I'd like to do before I die is to see the sea again. I'd like to see the sun shining on the water – the way we used to from the cliffs at Northcote Mouth. Do you remember?'

'Yes.' Rupert half turned to look at her. 'I should think that could be managed. Northcote Mouth is a bit far, but we might go down to Brighton for the day.'

'Not Brighton, I think – not in your present circumstances.'

'Not Brighton itself then. The Downs – Beachy Head perhaps.'

'But not on those awful motorways – I don't care for rushing along with no view. I want to see the countryside – slowly, as we did in the old days.'

'That should be possible. I'll get out the maps. We'll plot a route. . . .' He smiled and murmured to himself, '. . . to Paradise, by way of Beachy Head.'

'What, dear?'

'We'll hire a car – with a chauffeur – a big one, a Humber or a Daimler with a glass partition, so we can sit in the back and look out grandly on the old world.'

'I don't want to be grand.'

'Not grand then – comfortable . . . comfortably ourselves. We can. . . .' His attention was caught by a movement in the road beyond the gate – a car, the slam of a car door.

He leant forward and suddenly Miranda appeared and pushed open the gate. She stood for a moment, her dark hair gleaming under the light, and then began to walk very slowly towards the back door.

'May, I think I'll just take the tea things into the kitchen.'

'Is that tea?' she said, staring at the trolley.

Rupert shut the back door. 'It was. Do you want tea? I'll make a new pot.'

'Not really,' she said vaguely.

He came close to her. 'What's . . . happened?'

'Happened?'

'Oliver – Grandad – how is he?'

'Grandad? Oh – Grandad's dead.'

'Ah. . . .' He rubbed his face. 'When did he . . . it must have been quick?'

'Quick – no, not quick.' She frowned, keeping her eyes averted. 'A long time. A long, long time. Nearly all the way to the hospital.'

'Tell me about it, Milly.'

'Well,' she said tonelessly, 'they put the stretcher in the ambulance. And I got in with him and one of the orderlies got in. And then we started off – quite fast with the siren going. And then just before we arrived, he died.'

'Did he – regain consciousness?'

She gave a tight little nod.

'Tell me,' he said quietly, 'please. . . .'

'Well,' she took a deep breath, 'he came t-to almost at once. I think the siren disturbed him. He said, "What's this – where am I?" I said, "It's alright, Grandad, you're in the ambulance." "Where's Rupert?" he said. I told him you were at home with Granny. He'd been staring at the roof of the ambulance, but then he turned his head a bit and looked at me – and he saw the orderly, and I think he took it in then. His lips sort of trembled and he said, "I want May – I can't leave May all alone." And then the wretched orderly said, "Alright, Dad, just relax, we'll be there in a jiffy." And Grandad said, "But I don't want to go anywhere" – and he began to cry – l-like a little child and he made a kind of movement as though he wanted to get up, and the orderly leaned forward and started to pull the sponge away – he'd been clutching the sponge all the time, you see – I suppose he wanted to make him more comfortable or something. And Grandad said, "No no no no! May," he said, "May" – and I pushed past the orderly and took his hand – the other hand, not the sponge hand and – and. . . .' Miranda wept.

'There there, my poppet,' he took her into his arms, 'my little love. . . .'

'Oh Poopa, he was frightened – he was so frightened. . . .'

'Sssh – my angel love, my sweetheart. . . .'

She sobbed softly. 'The tears were rolling down his cheeks and he was trembling and he looked like a sort of terribly sad old dog . . . a bloodhound or. . . .' She gave a little hiccoughing laugh.

Rupert said, 'He never liked dogs.'

'No, I know. He used to kick them, didn't he?' She drew back her head to look at her father.

'And then?'

'Well – after a bit he seemed to calm down and closed his eyes. Then just as we turned into the hospital gates, he opened them again and gave a little burp and said, "Ah" – and smiled the way a baby smiles after a . . . and then. . . .' She looked away. 'And then he was dead.'

Rupert touched her chin and turned her head back to him. He took out a crumpled handkerchief and carefully dried her tears.

'Thank you, Poopa.' She stepped back and unbuckled her raincoat. From the pocket she brought out the sponge and set it on the table.

Rupert smiled faintly. 'Well, he didn't give that up so easily.'

Miranda shook her head and put a small envelope next to the sponge. She slipped off the coat.

'What's that?'

'Dr Oldfield brought me back – he gave me some Valium in case May needed it.'

'I see. We'd better go and tell her.'

Miranda ran her fingers through her hair. 'Alright,' she said, taking his hand, 'I'm ready.'

'Is it all over?'

'Yes, Granny, it's all over.'

May reached up and caught hold of Miranda's hand. 'Was he very frightened?'

Miranda darted a questioning glance at Rupert, who nodded. 'He was a bit frightened, yes,' she said.

May sighed. 'He was frightened about so many things. I never really understood why.'

Miranda said, 'He wanted you – asked for you.'

'I expect so.' She patted Miranda's hand, then released it. 'That's what he liked, you know – for me to be there. I don't know what for. I don't know what good I ever did him. . . . Poor old gentleman, he wouldn't have liked to peg out in the back of an ambulance. He wanted to die with fanfare and trumpets. Still, we can't all have what we want all the time, can we?'

'There'll be a memorial service,' said Rupert. 'He can have trumpets then.'

'A memorial service – oh dear, oh dear. Shall I have to go?'

'Not if you –'

' –because I honestly don't think I'm up to it.'

'Then of course you don't,' Rupert said firmly. 'You don't have to do anything unless you want to.'

'Oh. Does that mean I won't have to go into hospital?'

Miranda exchanged a startled glance with Rupert and then said, 'Of course, it's up to you, Granny, but –'

'I've never very much cared for the idea, as you know, and really it hardly seems necessary now. After all, I shan't be going upstairs anymore, shall I?'

'Oh.' He took out a cigarette. 'Won't you?'

'No, dear – I shall follow your very sensible suggestion and sleep downstairs in future. The daybed in the studio will suit me very well, it's really quite comfortable – or used to be.'

Miranda said, 'Have you been in the studio lately, Granny?'

'No, I can't say I have; I expect you mean it's rather a mess?'

'Well – yes, it is.'

'That doesn't surprise me – he hasn't let Vi in there in a month of Sundays, but we can soon . . . oh blow! Vi! Vi will have to be told. . . .'

'I'll see to that,' Rupert said quickly.

'Would you, dear? I should be grateful. She's a dear good body, but I honestly don't think I could face a lot of weeping and wailing just at the moment.' She closed her eyes for a moment.

'I'll give her a ring right away.'

May mutely shook her head.

'In the morning then?'

'Yes, dear.' She cleared her throat. 'You'd better do it first thing – before she starts on her way up. I shouldn't like her to walk unawares into a. . . .'

'No, of course not.' Rupert lit his cigarette. 'May, would you like a drop more whisky in your glass?'

'No thank you, dear.'

Miranda said, 'Or a Valium perhaps?'

'Valium?'

'A tranquilizer,' Miranda said awkwardly, 'you know – to calm you down.'

'I hardly think I need a pill for that, my dear. After all, I'm likely to have all the tranquility I need from now on, aren't I?'

Rupert smiled. 'Well, I could do with a drink. I expect you could too, Milly?'

'Yes, alright, Poopa. And I'll attend to the fire.' She knelt down and began to jab at the coals with the poker.

'And Rupert,' May said, when he came back with the glasses, 'I think you'd better write to those stairlift people in the morning and cancel Oliver's order. I shan't have any use for a stairlift now.'

'Yes, alright – and I'll ring *The Times* too, they'll be wanting to put in an obituary.'

'Oh really, Daddy!' Miranda said, standing up and taking her glass.

'No, he's quite right, my dear,' May nodded approval. 'And you should get in contact with the local paper as well – they've always thought very highly of Oliver and I'm sure they'll want to give him plenty of space. He designed the new municipal lavatories, you know.'

Miranda took a quick drink.

'Now, my dear,' May said, easing herself forward and reaching back for her cane, 'I'll trouble you to give me a hand up – if you've finished your whisky, that is.'

Miranda drained her glass and put it on the mantelpiece. 'Here we are.' She held out her hand.

'Just a gentle pull . . . that's it. We'd better go and see whether Vi has kept the daybed made up. I don't suppose she has for a minute, in which case I'll have to ask you to pop upstairs and get some linen from the airing cupboard – and the quilt from my bed and the eiderdown and, oh, perhaps an extra blanket. The studio has always been a chilly room, facing north as it does.'

Rupert watched their gentle progress across the room to the far door. What was she going to make of the Pyramid?

'Rupert, you'll take care of the locking up and all that sort of thing, won't you?'

'Yes, don't worry, I'll look after it.'

He put down his glass and warmed his hands at the fire. It was cold; the brief flirtation with summer was over. He went over to the window and looked out at the night and his own image reflected by the glass. Slowly he reached up and took hold of the blind-pull – 'What, warder, ho! Let the portcullis fall!' he said, and pulled down the blind.